Acclaim for Colleen Coble

"Second chances, old flames, and startling new revelations combine to form a story filled with faith, trial, forgiveness, and redemption. Crack the cover and step in, but beware—Mermaid Point is harboring secrets that will keep you guessing."

—Lisa Wingate, national bestselling author of *The Sea Keeper's Daughters* on *Mermaid Moon*

"I burned through *The Inn at Ocean's Edge* in one sitting. An intricate plot by a master storyteller. Colleen Coble has done it again with this gripping opening to a new series. I can't wait to spend more time at Sunset Cove."

—Heather Burch, bestselling author of *One Lavender Ribbon*

"Coble doesn't disappoint with her custom blend of suspense and romance."

—*Publishers Weekly* for *The Inn at Ocean's Edge*

"Veteran author Coble has penned another winner. Filled with mystery and romance that are unpredictable until the last page, this novel will grip readers long past when they should put their books down. Recommended to readers of contemporary mysteries."

—*CBA Retailers + Resources* review of *The Inn at Ocean's Edge*

"Coble truly shines when she's penning a mystery, and this tale will really keep the reader guessing . . . Mystery lovers will definitely want to put this book on their purchase list."

—*Romantic Times* Book Review of *The Inn at Ocean's Edge*

"Master storyteller Colleen Coble has done it again. *The Inn at Ocean's Edge* is an intricately woven, well-crafted story of romance, suspense, family secrets, and a decades old mystery. Needless to say, it had me hooked from page one. I simply couldn't stop turning the pages. This one's going on my keeper shelf."

—Lynette Eason, award-winning, bestselling author of the Hidden Identity series

"Evocative and gripping, *The Inn at Ocean's Edge* will keep you flipping pages long into the night."

—Dani Pettrey, bestselling author of the Alaskan Courage series

"Coble's atmospheric and suspenseful series launch should appeal to fans of Tracie Peterson and other authors of Christian romantic suspense."

—*Library Journal* review of *Tidewater Inn*

"Romantically tense, but with just the right touch of danger, this cowboy love story is surprisingly clever—and pleasingly sweet."

—USAToday.com review of *Blue Moon Promise*

"Colleen Coble will keep you glued to each page as she shows you the beauty of God's most primitive land and the dangers it hides."

—www.RomanceJunkies.com

"[An] outstanding, completely engaging tale that will have you on the edge of your seat . . . A must-have for all fans of romantic suspense!"

—TheRomanceReadersConnection.com review of *Anathema*

"Colleen Coble lays an intricate trail in *Without a Trace* and draws the reader on like a hound with a scent."

—*Romantic Times*, 4½ stars

"Coble's historical series just keeps getting better with each entry."

—*Library Journal* starred review of *The Lightkeeper's Ball*

"Don't ever mistake [Coble's] for the fluffy romances with a little bit of suspense. She writes solid suspense, and she ties it all together beautifully with a wonderful message."

—LifeinReviewBlog.com review of *Lonestar Angel*

"This book has everything I enjoy: mystery, romance, and suspense. The characters are likable, understandable, and I can relate to them."

—TheFriendlyBookNook.com

"[M]ystery, danger, and intrigue as well as romance, love, and subtle inspiration. *The Lightkeeper's Daughter* is a 'keeper.'"

—OnceUponaRomance.com

"Colleen is a master storyteller."

—Karen Kingsbury, bestselling author of *Unlocked* and *Learning*

The Heart Answers

Also by Colleen Coble

Sunset Cove novels
The Inn at Ocean's Edge
Mermaid Moon
Twilight at Blueberry Barrens
(Available September 2016)

Hope Beach novels
Tidewater Inn
Rosemary Cottage
Seagrass Pier
All Is Bright: A Hope Beach Christmas Novella (e-book only)

Under Texas Stars novels
Blue Moon Promise
Safe in His Arms

The Mercy Falls series
The Lightkeeper's Daughter
The Lightkeeper's Bride
The Lightkeeper's Ball

Lonestar novels
Lonestar Sanctuary
Lonestar Secrets
Lonestar Homecoming
Lonestar Angel
All Is Calm: A Lonestar Christmas Novella (e-book only)

The Rock Harbor series
Without a Trace
Beyond a Doubt
Into the Deep
Cry in the Night
Silent Night: A Rock Harbor Christmas Novella (e-book only)

The Aloha Reef series
Distant Echoes
Black Sands
Dangerous Depths
Midnight Sea
Holy Night: An Aloha Reef Christmas Novella (e-book only)

Alaska Twilight
Fire Dancer
Abomination
Anathema
Butterfly Palace

Novellas included in:
Smitten
Secretly Smitten
Smitten Book Club

Other Novellas
Bluebonnet Bride

The Heart Answers

A Novel

COLLEEN COBLE

THOMAS NELSON
Since 1798

Published in Nashville, Tennessee, by Thomas Nelson. Thomas Nelson is a registered trademark of HarperCollins Christian Publishing, Inc.

Thomas Nelson titles may be purchased in bulk for educational, business, fund-raising, or sales promotional use. For information, please e-mail SpecialMarkets@ThomasNelson.com.

Publisher's Note: This novel is a work of fiction. Names, characters, places, and incidents are either products of the author's imagination or used fictitiously. All characters are fictional, and any similarity to people living or dead is purely coincidental.

Library of Congress Cataloging-in-Publication Data

Names: Coble, Colleen, author.
Title: The heart answers / Colleen Coble.
Description: Nashville, Tennessee: Thomas Nelson, [2016]
Identifiers: LCCN 2015050413 | ISBN 9780529103444 (paperback)
Subjects: | GSAFD: Love stories. | Christian fiction.
Classification: LCC PS3553.O2285 H423 2016 | DDC 813/.54—dc23 LC record available at http://lccn.loc.gov/2015050413

Printed in the United States of America

16 17 18 19 20 RRD 6 5 4 3 2 1

For my parents, George and Peggy Rhoads, who have always believed I could do anything. Thanks for always being there for me.

One

March 1867

Fort Phil Kearny, Wyoming Territory

"You're what?" Jessica DuBois raised her normally well-modulated voice to a near shriek.

"A lady never raises her voice, dear." Her mother blotted a few crumbs of toast and jam from her lips and rose to her feet. "Your uncle Samuel is alone with three young children who need a mother. You and I need a home, and Samuel has graciously offered us one. I haven't wanted to worry you, but I really was at my wit's end when I learned there would be so little money for us to live on."

"But what about Boston?" Jessica jumped to her feet and nearly tripped over her blue wool gown. She yanked at it. How could she be so clumsy? "Papa has only been dead a little over two months. How can you even think about marrying another man so quickly? What would Papa say?"

Her mother cupped Jessica's cheek. "He would be glad you and I were provided for. Now I really must pack. The troop leaves in two days, and I promised Samuel we would get to Fort Bridger as soon as we could."

Jessica watched as her mother gathered her skirt in her hand and swished from the kitchen. Fort Bridger! She wanted the bright lights of Boston, concerts, social life, and teas with her friends.

What friends? She shrugged the thought away. Her mother couldn't do this to her. She didn't want to be buried in some backwater ever again. She'd had all she could stand of soldiers and dust and months-old news. *And humiliation.* She was desperate to get away from the stares of censure.

Unable to remain still, she walked to the front window and looked out on Fort Phil Kearny's snow-covered parade ground. The March sunshine was beginning to melt some of the snow, but the incessant wind still poked icy fingers into everything. A few soldiers bent into the gale as they hurried to the warmth of the sutler's store across the way.

She would be glad to get out of this place. She didn't want to run into Rand Campbell or Isaac Liddle ever again. Both men had eventually thrown her over for other women. And she hated the pity in their wives' eyes whenever they met. Emmie Liddle, in particular, irritated her beyond all reason.

Her eyes widened as she thought about the situation. Why couldn't she go to Boston without her mother? She could stay with her aunt, as distasteful as that might be.

She hurried across the hall and interrupted her mother's packing. "I'm going to stay with Aunt Penelope."

Her mother sighed and turned to face her. "I'm sorry, dear, but that just is not possible."

"Why not?" Jessica's throat tightened and she swallowed. She had to get out of here.

Her mother bit her lip. "There just isn't enough money to send you back to Boston. I'm afraid your father left us quite destitute." She put her hand to her mouth. "Perhaps by spring I can save enough from your father's military pension to purchase a stage ticket."

"I can't go to Fort Bridger, Mama! I just can't!" She felt near panic at the thought of continuing to live in this desert. Of continuing to face her ruined life here.

Her mother put out a placating hand. "I'm sure it won't be for long, darling. And Samuel says Fort Bridger is very pleasant. Lovely mountains, clear streams, and no dangerous natives. The only Indians he has seen since he arrived are friendly Shoshone. Please try to make the best of it."

Jessica pressed her lips together at her mother's implacable tone, then left her to pack. At least she'd be away from this fort, these people. She remembered the last time she had seen Uncle Samuel and his family. His children had teased her unmercifully, especially Miriam. She had poked fun at Jessica for being adopted.

She flinched at the painful memories, the nightmares that had plagued her for years. She would never forget the years of cold and hunger in the small shanty with her brother, Jasper.

One cold December night her mother had gone out partying and never returned. The police had come and taken Jasper and her away to an orphanage. She'd never seen her brother or her mother again.

Then her adoptive parents had arrived, taken one look at her beautiful face and red curls, and claimed her as their own. Papa had always told her he was a sucker for a beautiful woman. He'd made such a big thing of her beauty that she had always wondered if he would have picked her if she were plain. Even her beauty had been unable to save her from humiliation here.

Jessica threw herself across her bed and buried her face in her arms. She wanted to go to Boston. She needed activity to keep the memories at bay.

Two days later Jessica stood outside an army ambulance wagon with the wind and snow blowing about their well-guarded little convoy. The trip would be long and dangerous. Several of the wives and daughters had gathered to say good-bye to them.

Jessica glimpsed Sarah Campbell and Emmie Liddle and turned her head. She didn't want to have to speak to them, but she didn't have any choice. Sarah touched her arm, and Jessica steeled herself to face them. Both Sarah and Emmie wore identical expressions of concern.

"Jessica, I just wanted to ask you to forgive me for any hurt I've caused you in the past," Sarah said.

"Me too," Emmie put in. "We don't want to part as enemies. We just want you to know that we'll be praying for you."

Jessica narrowed her eyes and stared at them. Pray for her? Did they think they were so much better than an orphanage foundling that their prayers mattered more than her own? "I don't need your prayers. I'll be just fine." She pointedly turned away from them as other ladies came to say good-bye.

She clenched a fist in the folds of her skirt, then gathered her skirts and climbed into the ambulance. She glanced back at Emmie and Sarah. Good. They were gone. How dare they sit in judgment on her. Pray for her, indeed. She didn't need any prayers, especially from them. She was beautiful, and she would make her own way in the world.

Clay Cole reined in Misty, his bay mare, and looked back over the trail he had just covered. The wind tried to tease his wide-brimmed hat from his head, but it was jammed on too tightly. He took out his red bandanna and wiped his face and neck. After traveling mostly at night, he was nearly to Fort Caspar. Now he could finally travel in the light of day. Most of the Sioux were north, terrorizing the forts along the Bozeman Trail. Throughout the entire year of 1866, they had carried out a war against forts like Phil Kearny and C. F. Smith farther north into Montana. The region had buzzed with the news of over eighty men slaughtered at Fort Phil Kearny two and a half months ago.

He yawned and stretched his cramped muscles, then turned his mare's head into the wind and started down the trail again. At least the spring thaw had set in early this year. A few days ago the snow had begun to melt, though the wind still blew. He rounded a curve and came to a sudden halt.

The sound of shots and shrieks made him dig his heels into his mare's flank and pull his rifle loose. About a dozen Indians circled an army train just ahead. The soldiers had formed a protective circle and were firing methodically at the war tribe. Clay let out a whoop of his own and shot his rifle into the air.

A fearsomely painted Sioux turned. At Clay's thundering approach, he wheeled around, signaling to his band to retreat. Clay knew they thought he was bringing reinforcements. He howled again, and his charge scattered the last of the Sioux. He reined in Misty, then cantered into the circle of wagons.

A young woman with red curls peered from the back of an ambulance, and he waved at her. After a moment she gave a hesitant wave, then withdrew back inside the ambulance.

A young lieutenant with thin brown hair cantered up to him. "Howdy, Preacher. You showed up in the nick of time. I was a bit surprised you fired on them, though. Thought you didn't believe in violence."

Clay grinned. "I can fight when I have to, Tom. Today wasn't one of those times. I just gave them a good excuse to leave."

The lieutenant raised his eyebrows. "Well, it worked. Thanks."

"Thank God, Tom."

He reddened and cut his gaze to the left of Clay's ear. "You can do the praying, Preacher. I don't have the knack for it." He turned his horse's head and galloped back to the front of the wagon train.

Clay watched him go with a rueful grin. He'd been witnessing to Tom Harris for over a year now. Clay was discouraged that he wasn't seeing more fruit from his ministry yet. But here was where the Lord had called him, and here he would stay unless God decreed otherwise.

He fell into line with the convoy, and the remainder of the trip into Fort Caspar was uneventful. The wind cut through his coat in spite of the weak sunshine, and Clay longed for the warmth of a fire and a hot cup of coffee.

Just before dusk he saw the smoke spiraling from Fort Caspar ahead and breathed a sigh. He knew the soldiers felt the same relief. He wondered briefly about the young woman he'd seen in the ambulance. What was she doing traveling in the middle of March? Perhaps she'd lost a husband recently. He made a mental note to check on her tomorrow and offer her some comfort from God's Word.

The mess hall was crowded when he made his way inside. He heard a shout and turned to see a young tornado running across the room. "Uncle Clay!" Three-year-old Franny hurtled toward him. She always called him uncle, although they were actually cousins.

He swung her into his arms and searched for Franny's parents, Ellen and Martin. Ellen sat near the stove, and he made his way to her side with Franny clinging to his neck.

Ellen rose with a gentle smile. "I didn't expect to see you back from Montana so quickly. But I'm glad you're here." Her words were low and choked with emotion.

Clay searched her eyes, and his heart jumped at the grief he found there. "What's happened?" He didn't think he really wanted to hear the answer.

Ellen swallowed hard and her lips trembled. "Martin was killed in a skirmish last week."

Clay went very still. He and Martin were first cousins, but their relationship had always been that of brothers. He tried to speak past the tightness in his throat, but all that came out was a clicking sound.

Ellen touched his arm. "Let's go to our quarters. I shouldn't have blurted it out like that."

A few minutes later he was seated at their kitchen table with a cup of steaming coffee in his trembling hand and Franny on his knee. His eyes blurring, he stared into the dark liquid and tried to get his thoughts around the fact of Martin's death. He would never see Martin's gap-toothed smile again, or the way his hair stuck up in a funny cowlick. Clay raised his head and looked into Ellen's grief-stricken eyes. "What will you and Franny do now?"

She breathed out a heavy sigh. "I really don't know. I have to vacate these quarters next week. I suppose I could go home, but I love it out here. I can't quite bear the thought of going back to Indiana and leaving Martin in the cemetery on the hill. If I could just find some kind of job, I'd stay." She gave him a tremulous smile. "I even asked about taking on the post laundry, but Major Larson wouldn't hear of it. Maybe at another fort where no one knew Martin I'd have better luck."

"I could get you on at Bridger." He hated to see her take on such a hard task, but there weren't many jobs around for women. Not decent women anyway. At least at Bridger he could check on Ellen and Franny occasionally.

Ellen immediately brightened. "Oh, Clay, that would be wonderful!"

Before he could respond, someone knocked on the door. Ellen rose and hurried to see who it was. The wind howled through the open door and nearly knocked over the two women standing in the doorway.

"Oh, you poor dears. Come in by the fire." Ellen ushered them inside and took their wraps.

Clay raised his eyebrows at the sight of the young woman he'd seen in the back of the ambulance. Big blue eyes shone from a face with skin so translucent it looked like porcelain. But Clay was immune to her lustrous red curls and shapely figure. If he ever married, he wanted a woman with a beautiful inner character who wasn't consumed by her looks the way his mother had been. Still, he glimpsed a vulnerability in her beautiful eyes that intrigued him. What was her story?

Jessica was so glad to be out of the ambulance with her feet on solid ground, she didn't even mind the rude accommodations. The tiny cabin was hardly any bigger than her bedroom back in Fort Phil Kearny, but it was warm and homey and smelled wonderfully of coffee and yeast from the fresh bread on the table. Her mouth watered at the aroma.

Her gaze traveled to the figure standing behind their hostess, and her eyes widened. It was the same man who had driven off the Indians earlier in the day. He was very tall, with massive arms, broad shoulders, dark hair, and hazel eyes above a Roman nose. He held a tiny blonde girl, and she felt a pang of disappointment at the thought that the child might be his. If he was unattached, he might be a pleasant diversion for the evening. She sent him a tiny smile, but he just responded with a polite nod.

Her mother fluttered her hands. "My dear Mrs. Branson, we do so apologize for barging in this way. Major Larson assured us that you were used to taking in strays. We do beg your hospitality. I'm Letty DuBois and this is my daughter, Jessica."

Jessica fixed her eyes on Ellen and smiled. "I wouldn't turn down some of that fragrant coffee." Why did her mother always sound so apologetic?

Letty bobbed her head. "Your coffee does smell wonderful. The aroma called to us on the porch."

Ellen gestured to the table. "Please, sit down and I'll bring you both a cup of coffee and some bread. It's still warm." She led the way to the kitchen and grabbed two coffee cups, both chipped around the rim. "This is Clay Cole and my daughter. Say hello, Franny."

"'Lo," the little girl mumbled. Her eyes were round as she stared at Jessica. She wiggled, and Clay set her on the floor. She hesitantly drew closer to Jessica and touched the soft material of her gown. "You're pretty."

A bit at a loss, Jessica had never had another female besides her mother compliment her, not even one as tiny as this one. "Thank you. So are you." She was surprised to find she meant those words. The little girl looked angelic with her soft blonde curls tied back in a blue bow and her big blue eyes round with admiration.

Franny's eyes grew even bigger. "I am?"

Jessica nodded. "Very pretty. Would you like to sit on my lap?" She wanted to catch the words back as soon as she spoke them. What if the child had jam on her fingers? But it was too late to back down now. Even Mama looked surprised as Franny climbed onto Jessica's lap and settled there contentedly.

How comforting the warmth of that small body felt pressed against her. She'd never had time for children. Actually, she'd never been around many small children. She awkwardly shifted Franny into the crook of her arm and took the coffee Ellen handed her.

"What brings the two of you to Fort Caspar?" Ellen asked.

Mama glanced sideways at Jessica. "We're on our way to Fort Bridger. My husband died in the Fetterman disaster, and I'm going to care for his brother's children."

Jessica put down her cup on the rough table. "Tell them the truth, Mama. You're marrying another man, and my father isn't even cold in his grave yet." She choked on the last sentence. How could Mama be so heartless? Had she really even loved Papa?

Jessica looked down at the child on her lap. What was love anyway? A temporary madness that enabled a woman to get a man to do what she wanted. She doubted if there was such a thing as a love that withstood any kind of disruption.

She eyed Clay surreptitiously through her partially lowered lashes. He was quite good looking. A fine male specimen actually. He wasn't in uniform, so he wasn't a soldier. Perhaps he was a settler or a guide? It didn't really matter. All that mattered was that he wasn't married to Ellen. A mild flirtation would relieve the boredom. Jessica glanced at Ellen but dismissed her as competition. She was short and pudgy with thin, flyaway brown hair and a mouth too wide for her face.

"Do you live here at Fort Caspar?" she asked Clay.

He shook his head. "Just passing through on my way to Bridger."

Before Jessica could respond, Franny slid to the floor. "Uncle Clay, you haven't seen my new dolly. Daddy gave it to me." She took his hand and tugged. "Come see."

"Okay, angel face," he said with an indulgent smile. "Show me your dolly."

"May I come too?" What a perfect opportunity to get Clay to herself.

Franny nodded. "But you can't hold her. Only Mommy and me can hold her." She led the way to a tiny room, more a closet than a bedroom, with a small bed pushed up against the wall. She picked up a rag doll from the bed and held it up proudly. "This is Molly."

Clay squatted in front of the little girl. "She's very pretty, Franny. But not as pretty as you, because you're beautiful inside where only Jesus can see."

Jesus? Jessica eyed him, then admired the doll too. She sidled closer to Clay. "I'm so glad you'll be going to Fort Bridger. I do hope you'll find the time to come see me after we arrive. I'd really like to get to know the brave man who saved us from the Indians." She laid a hand on his shoulder and gave him a tiny smile that showed her perfect white teeth to advantage.

Clay looked up at her for a moment, then gently pried her hand from his shoulder. "Don't waste your wiles on me, Miss DuBois. I'm sure there are plenty of men in Bridger who will be glad to dance attendance on you. I have better things to do." He swept Franny up into his arms, then strode from the room without a backward glance.

"You, you–" How dare he speak to her like that! She put her hands to her hot cheeks. No man had ever snubbed her before in her entire life. There had been men who had walked away later, but never a man who had been immune to her beauty right from the first meeting.

She swallowed her anger and assumed a distant smile. He mustn't see that his words had bothered her one bit. She'd had years of practice at hiding pain and disappointment. No backwoods cowboy was going to have the satisfaction of hurting her now. She took a deep breath and strode back into the kitchen.

Everyone was seated at the table once again, chattering animatedly.

"Oh, there you are, dear. I was just telling Ellen she must travel in the ambulance with us tomorrow. It will be so pleasant to have another woman to talk to."

"You're going to Bridger?" Jessica sat back down in her chair without a glance at Clay. "Is your husband being transferred?"

A look of pain passed over Ellen's face. "My husband was killed last week," she said quietly. "Clay is arranging for me to work at Fort Bridger."

Uh-oh. Maybe she was competition after all. Not that Jessica cared after the way Clay had talked to her. But what satisfaction there would be to have Clay Cole eating out of her hand before she tossed him over. She knew exactly what she would say too. "But, Clay, dear, you can't possibly want to marry a beautiful woman. You have better things to do. Run along and see if Ellen will have you. I certainly won't."

Jessica was so lost in her pleasant daydream of crushing Clay under her heel that she missed what else Ellen had to say about her job. "That's nice," she said absently. "We'll be glad to have you to tea when we get settled."

Both her mother and Clay gave her strange glances. What was wrong with them? She fixed a bright smile on her face. "Franny can spend some time with me while you're working."

"You'll be much too busy to bother with Franny." Ellen let out a nervous laugh. "She can help me with the laundry."

Laundry? Ellen did her own laundry? How odd. But Jessica was too full of plans to humiliate Clay to give it much thought. *Revenge* was such a sweet word.

Two

Over the next few days, Jessica did not find much opportunity to put her plans into action. She only caught occasional glimpses of Clay when she got out of the ambulance to stretch her legs and walk.

Ellen and Franny often joined her, and she found herself relaxing in Ellen's company. She'd never had a friend before. She didn't trust women, and she trusted men even less. But Ellen was different. She didn't seem to have a bad word to say about anyone. She always had time to listen to her little girl, and she shared her thoughts and feelings with Jessica. Jessica still hadn't shared anything meaningful about herself, but it was pleasant to feel as though she could and Ellen would keep her confidences private. Maybe someday she would tell Ellen about her childhood.

One bright morning Jessica saw Clay walking his mare behind the ambulance. He didn't seem in any hurry to leave, so she decided it was a perfect opportunity to pique his interest. Sunshine enhanced the sheen of her red hair, so she loosened the ribbon that tied it back and climbed out the back of the wagon.

Clay looked up with a wary expression as she fell into step beside him. "Where is Ellen?"

"Taking a nap with Franny. She needs the rest. Martin's loss has been hard on her."

"I'm surprised someone like you would notice."

Jessica bristled. "Like me? You have no idea what I'm like. We only exchanged a few words, and that was days ago. What makes you think you know anything about me?" She quickly erased her scowl. Why did the man bring out the worst in her?

He smiled. "It certainly looks as though you've had everything you've ever wanted. Riches, adoration. I'm not the kind of man a woman like you would normally notice."

Rich. If he only knew. But still, at least he was talking to her. "My father didn't leave us much money." She tossed her head, and his eyes strayed to her cascading hair.

Clay raised his eyebrows, and his smile widened. "Oh? A little poverty is good for the soul. You might learn something." He broke off when a soldier from the front of the procession hailed him. He swung up onto his mare and cantered away without a backward glance.

Jessica gritted her teeth and stared after him. She had to figure out what he admired in a woman. She looked toward the back of the ambulance. Maybe when Ellen awakened they would have a little talk about "cousin" Clay.

Hoping he might come back, she walked along a few more minutes, then climbed back into the ambulance. Ellen and Franny were both awake and chatting with Jessica's mother. Jessica tied the canvas flap in place and joined them on the seats along the walls of the wagon.

"Your cheeks are pink, dear. I do wish you'd take your parasol when you're out in this bright sun. Your skin will burn if you're not careful."

Jessica shrugged at her mother. "I forgot it. Ellen, I saw Clay just now. He seems so aloof, and I was wondering about his background."

Ellen laughed. "Clay, aloof? You just don't know him well enough yet. He's actually Martin's cousin, you know, and he's been a good friend to me. Whenever he passes through our area, he always spends a few days with us."

"Has he ever married?"

"Not Clay. He doesn't think it would be fair to ask a woman to share his nomadic life. But he is attractive, isn't he? He wouldn't have any trouble finding a wife, if he were so inclined."

Just then the shout of "Bridger ahead!" brought their conversation to an end.

Her mother lurched to her feet and patted her head. "Oh my. My hair is a rat's nest. What will Samuel think?"

"You look fine, Mama. Uncle Samuel isn't expecting a fashion plate after a trip across the wilderness." Jessica grabbed her ribbon, tied her hair back, then sighed and clasped her hands in her lap. Another fort. Each one was almost like the last one, and it was such a boring life. Why couldn't she be looking forward to parties in Boston instead of dealing with her cousins in Wyoming Territory?

The ambulance wagon lurched to a halt, and moments later

she heard Uncle Samuel's familiar gruff voice. He sounded so much like her father that her eyes stung. Life was so unfair. Why couldn't it be Papa's voice outside the wagon? *Why, why, why?* The unsettling questions had no answers.

Her mother hurried to untie the canvas flap at the back of the wagon, and Samuel climbed aboard. He smelled of fresh air, tobacco, and the cloves he was always sucking. His broad shoulders made the tiny space seem even smaller. The lump in her throat grew larger because her uncle had the same silky, dark hair and square-jawed face her father had had. Her father's jawline had enhanced his air of authority, while Uncle Samuel's jaw was a bit softer. He looked genial, prosperous, and good-natured.

And why shouldn't he look good-natured? Jessica sniffed. He was getting her mother as a drudge to cook and clean and take care of his brood. But not her. *She* wasn't about to kowtow to a man like that. She couldn't imagine a worse fate than laundry and cooking and cleaning up after other people.

"I've been watching the horizon for days," Samuel said in a hearty voice. "The kids are excited too."

Jessica bit her upper lip to prevent it from curling. If she knew Miriam, she wasn't any more eager to spend time together than Jessica was. She gazed past her uncle's burly form, but all she could see were milling soldiers and rough log cabins. Where were the cousins anyway? She and her mother gathered their possessions and handed them to Samuel.

He turned and bellowed out the back of the ambulance wagon, "Caleb!"

Jessica's eyebrows raised as her cousin Caleb appeared. At fifteen he was already taller than his father and looked nothing like the eight-year-old boy she remembered. He was scrawny, but with the promise of slender good looks to come. He nodded to her and her mother, then stood and accepted the bundles from his father.

"Where are your sisters?" Samuel demanded. "They should be here to greet their new family."

Caleb shrugged. "Miriam said something about baking bread, and Bridie was reading."

Samuel sighed. "You'll have to take them in hand, Letty. They've been on their own too long and don't mind the niceties much."

Mama nodded. "I shall enjoy it, Samuel. We always wanted more children." She glanced at Jessica and fell silent, then gave a cheery wave to Ellen and Franny. Samuel lifted her mother down from the wagon, and she smoothed her skirts and smiled up at him.

Jessica wanted to throw something and scream. How could her mother look with devotion at another man? Uncle Samuel might appear a bit like Papa, but he was a stranger to both of them. Her mother had only seen him two or three times and Jessica, only once. And that talk of wanting more children. Papa had always said Jessica was all the family they ever wanted. But the comment brought up memories of Jasper, and she swallowed hard, her throat tight.

She followed them slowly and looked around. Fort Bridger had neat log cabins laid out around the usual parade ground, where the soldiers practiced their maneuvers and gathered for roll call. The river gurgling through the center of this parade ground was a bit unusual. Across the way she could see the warren of trade establishments. A couple of emigrants argued with a short, stocky blacksmith, and farther down several horses milled in the stable. A wagon train sat curled in its circle of protection just beyond the fort proper. Perhaps more than just soldiers would be here. Ellen had told her that Bridger was a favorite stopping-off place for emigrants on their way farther west.

"Where are our quarters, Samuel?" Mama asked in a timid voice.

He hesitated. "If you're agreeable, I thought we would be married this afternoon, and you and Jessica could move in right away."

Mama blushed and bobbed her head. "Is there a preacher on the grounds?"

"Supposed to be one come in with you. I'll go check and see if he arrived."

Jessica waited until his broad back disappeared around a wagon, then turned to her mother. "Don't let him railroad you into a hasty marriage. You don't even know him all that well. He's not Papa. I want to spend a little time in our own place before we move in with him."

Mama shot a sidelong glance at Caleb standing a few feet away, then whispered, "Don't make a scene, dear. I've already agreed to marry him. What difference does it make if the wedding takes place today or next week? I'm not going back on my word."

Jessica sighed and turned away. There was nothing more she

could say. But the minute she could, she was getting out of this place. She would put up with her uncle and cousins since she didn't have a choice at the moment, but surely it wouldn't be for long.

Samuel appeared a few minutes later. "The reverend is here. He'll come to our home in about an hour to perform the ceremony. Let's take your things to our quarters, and you can both freshen up."

They followed him across the parade ground. This fort didn't have the air of gloom that had hung over Fort Phil Kearny. Jessica glanced back toward the wagons and waved at Franny. The little girl started to run to her, but Ellen stopped her, then waved at Jessica too. Warmed by the exchange, Jessica squared her shoulders and prepared to meet Miriam and Bridie again.

The small home was surprisingly comfortable. The walls were lath and plaster, decorated with cheerful garden prints. A rug in soft greens and golds covered most of the floor. The fire blazed in the fireplace, and the aroma of some sort of stew greeted them as they stepped into the parlor.

Miriam sat on the sofa with her feet up. She looked up when they entered, then swung her feet to the floor. "So you're here." She turned and yelled down the hall, "Bridie! Aunt Letty and Jessica have arrived."

Miriam hadn't changed much. When Jessica looked into her cousin's almond-shaped gray eyes, she knew the old animosity still lingered. They were only a year apart in age, and Miriam had always been jealous of Jessica's beauty. Jessica gave a tiny sigh. She was too tired for her cousin's attitudes today, but she wasn't about to let her know. "Never give an inch to the enemy" was her motto. Put on a stiff upper lip, and don't let anyone see your weakness. But sometimes it got awfully lonely.

Bridie came in then, a pretty girl of thirteen with a wide smile and shiny brown hair. "Aunt Letty!" She kissed her warmly and turned to kiss Jessica. Jessica offered her cheek and stepped back quickly. She didn't like being touched by someone she didn't know well, though it was all right if *she* did the touching. Still, Bridie seemed nice enough. Better than Miriam, at any rate.

"You can freshen up in, uh, in our room," Samuel said hesitantly.

Mama blushed and Jessica gritted her teeth. Couldn't the man give her mother even a night or two on her own to get to know him? She followed her mother into the bedroom and closed the door behind them. She couldn't do anything about it, and she was just too tired to make any more objections tonight.

The small bedroom was furnished with a beautiful sleigh bed covered with a burgundy comforter. A hip bath hung on the wall, and several hooks for clothes were spaced around the room. Jessica took off her bonnet and shook her hair free. The curls were limp and dull from the dust of the trail. Thank goodness she wasn't seeing Clay again today. She ran a brush through her hair, then pinned it up again.

"Aren't you going to change your dress?" Mama asked when Jessica put on her bonnet.

"I just want to get this farce over with. I don't need to impress my dear *stepfather* or his horrid children. I'll wait until after the wedding for a good long soak." Her voice quivered, but she resolved not to cry.

"Whatever you say, dear."

Jessica glanced at her mother sharply and noticed her pale cheeks. "Are you all right, Mama?"

"Of course, of course." She turned her back to Jessica and began to unpack. "You go on out and get to know your new family a bit. I'll be right out."

My new family. Jessica would never consider them her family, and she would never feel close to any of them. She shut the door and entered the parlor. Never before had she shared her parents with anyone, not even a sibling, and she didn't want to share her mother now. She would have to find a way to get them away from Fort Bridger.

Bridie smiled when she entered and scooted over to make room for her on the sofa. Miriam gave her a disdainful look and gazed pointedly in the other direction. Jessica sat between her two cousins and smoothed her wrinkled skirt.

"Am I sleeping on the sofa?" She didn't see how there would be any room for her. Although comfortable, the quarters weren't large.

Samuel rubbed his hands together nervously. "Of course not, my dear. You'll share a room with Bridie and Miriam."

Jessica sucked in her breath and nearly groaned aloud. She hadn't considered that she might be in such close proximity to Miriam. How was she going to endure it until she could get out of this place? She had never shared a room in her life. She would have to endure Miriam's snipes after bedtime as well as before.

"The preacher should be here any minute. Is your mama about ready?" Samuel pulled out his pocket watch and peered at it. He raked a hand through his thick, dark hair.

Jessica nodded. "She said she'd be right out." His nervousness was obvious, but the fact didn't endear him to her. What did he have to be nervous about? She and her mother were the ones taking all the risk. Especially Mama.

Jessica jumped when the door knocker clattered. Samuel stopped his pacing and hurried to open the door. "Come in, Reverend." He stepped away from the door to allow the visitor to enter.

Jessica looked up and frowned when Clay came through the door, followed by Ellen and Franny.

"Jessie!" Franny ran to her and lifted her arms to be picked up.

Jessica lifted her onto her lap, but her eyes strayed to Clay's massive shoulders. Reverend? Clay was a *minister*? She couldn't believe it. She thought ministers were studious and soft-spoken. Clay was rugged and outspoken. He looked more like a lumberjack than a man of the cloth.

She pressed her lips together. Did his profession change her desire to humiliate him? It didn't. In fact, it added an extra fillip to the chase. Did a preacher fall as hard as an ordinary mortal? She looked down at her dust-stained dress, and her smile faded. Why hadn't she changed her clothes? She must look a dreadful sight.

The bedroom door opened, and her mother appeared. She gazed uncertainly around the parlor.

"The minister is here, my dear," Samuel said.

Mama glanced at Clay, then back to Samuel. "Oh dear." She bit her lip and wrung her hands. "Please forgive me, Reverend Clay–I mean, Reverend Cole. I had no idea you were a minister. I've not been addressing you properly the entire trip."

Clay delivered a reassuring smile. "I've always disliked being called Reverend. It makes me sound so pious and holy when I'm just a normal man like any other."

Jessica was going to prove just that.

"God has called me to preach his Word, but I fail him just as much as anyone else. Just call me Clay or even Preacher like the men do." Clay turned to Samuel. "Are you both ready, sir?"

Samuel nodded enthusiastically and reached out to draw Mama to his side.

Her mother swallowed hard, then took Samuel's hand. "I'm ready."

Jessica looked at her sharply and thought she saw tears in her mother's eyes. Her fingers curled into her palms, and she wanted to tear her mother's hand from her uncle's arm, then drag her from the house. She wanted to cry for her father and beg him to stop this travesty. But in the end, she did neither. She took her place beside her mother and listened to Clay's deep voice read the marriage vows.

Funny how she'd never really listened to the vows before. *Love, honor, cherish, obey. In sickness and in health. Till death do us part.* The words seemed so sacred and final. There was no way she would ever repeat those words and mean them. No man could be trusted to honor them.

She buried her face in Franny's silky hair and hugged her tightly. Her life had changed so much in the past few months, and she had never liked change. She'd had enough change in her childhood, being dragged from one roach-infested hovel to the next until she'd been taken in by her new parents. Predictability was her only security, but now as she looked toward the future, she had no idea what would happen next.

At the conclusion of the ceremony, Samuel bent his head and kissed his new wife. Jessica didn't like the gleam in his eye one bit. *What has Mama done?* Her uncle then turned to kiss her, and she offered up her cheek with reluctance.

"We're a family now. I want to take your father's place as much as I can."

Jessica managed a tight smile, but she couldn't say a word. Take Papa's place? How could he even suggest such an impossible thing? She turned away before she said anything hurtful. She couldn't stand the happy look on her mother's face, but she didn't want to spoil it either.

Clay was deep in conversation with Miriam, and a shaft of anger pierced Jessica. He snubbed her, then hung on Miriam's every word? The simpering smile on Miriam's face turned her stomach. Could Clay really like that kind of woman? She *was* beautiful, if you liked the pale, fragile type. Jessica forced a smile and sauntered over toward them.

"Miriam, dear, your father wants you to get the refreshments ready," she said in a sweet voice.

Miriam frowned at her, then flashed an adoring smile at Clay. "I'll talk to you later, Reverend Cole. Jessica and I have duties to attend to."

"Your father said you and Bridie," Jessica said casually.

"You're part of the family now too, *sister*." Miriam took her arm and practically dragged her to the kitchen.

Rather than struggle in front of Clay, Jessica allowed herself to be pulled away, but she clenched her hands into fists. She didn't like being touched.

"Don't you dare try to horn in now!" Miriam hissed once they were in the kitchen. "I saw him first."

"I don't think so, dear cousin." Jessica tossed her head. "Clay and I became very well acquainted on the trip here. Didn't you notice how Franny ran right to me?" She felt guilty about using the little girl, but this was war.

Miriam gave a tiny gasp. "Well, it doesn't matter. You stay out of my way." She flounced over to the table and cut slices of bread with jerky, fierce movements.

Jessica watched her for a moment, then shrugged and went back to the parlor. She wasn't about to let her cousin tell her what to do. Clay was standing beside Ellen with Franny in his arms, and the little girl reached out for Jessica when she approached. A strange look crossed Clay's face, but he handed Franny over to her.

"Why didn't you tell me you were a preacher?" Jessica went straight to the point.

"The subject never came up."

"I do so admire men of the cloth," she cooed. "I knew you were brave, but I didn't realize how brave."

He looked at her with surprise. "I'd think you would have

nothing but contempt for a minister. I don't even make enough money to keep you in hair ribbons."

Jessica tipped her chin up. "That just shows you how little you know me, but I intend to change that in the next few weeks." Out of the corner of her eye she saw Miriam scowling in the doorway.

His attention was important to her, more important than she could explain. But it was just a game, wasn't it?

Three

Clay saddled his mare and swung into the saddle. He'd been at Fort Bridger for a week and was getting itchy feet to move on to Colorado. He wanted to see how Private Lester Michaels was doing since he accepted the Lord two months ago. That was the bad thing about being an itinerant preacher–the constant worry about the spiritual condition of the men. They were sometimes like children, like the newborn babes the Bible called them, easily drawn back into their previous life of drinking and gambling. He knew how Paul had felt when he'd worried about the different churches. But it was all part of what God had called Clay to do.

He cantered out of the fort for a bit of exercise. Misty was feeling frisky this morning, too, and she broke into a run when they cleared the gates. He sniffed the early April air and took a deep fragrant breath of sage and creosote. He loved this land with a fierceness that surprised him. It was so different from Ohio, and at first he had missed the green hills and budding trees. Soon, though, he had come to love the starkness and strange beauty of this Great American Desert, as the papers called it.

He stopped under a lodgepole pine by a rock formation. There was a cave in the rock, and this was a favorite spot of his to spend some time with the Lord. He took his worn leather Bible and hunkered down on the rock. His Bible fell open to Matthew 7: "Judge not, that ye be not judged. For with what judgment ye judge, ye shall be judged: and with what measure ye mete, it shall be measured to you again. And why beholdest thou the mote that is in thy brother's eye, but considerest not the beam that is in thine own eye?"

Jessica's face came to mind and he frowned. What was it about her anyway? She seemed to dog his every step. He had no inclination to get tangled up with a woman like her. And yet there was something in her eyes that surprised him from time to time. Her lost-little-girl quality puzzled him.

His eyes turned back to the Scripture. Okay, so maybe he shouldn't judge Jessica too harshly. Maybe there was more to her background than he knew. But even as the thought crossed his mind, he dismissed it. She was just what she seemed: beautiful, spoiled, and willful. She had everything a woman could want, didn't she?

Except the Lord.

She wouldn't be interested, he argued with his inner conviction.

Have you really tried to show her real love, my love? Or have you been too eager to demonstrate how immune you are to her charms?

"She's dangerous, Lord," he said aloud.

She's a lost child. She needs me.

"All right, fine," Clay said. "I'll try, but don't expect too much."

I expect your all.

Clay bowed his head in resignation. The woman scared him for some reason, but it was his duty to do all he could to win her to Christ. It wouldn't be pleasant or easy, though.

After his prayer time he rode back to the fort and headed toward Ellen's quarters, where she was to begin her duties as post laundress today. He stifled a laugh. Had Jessica figured out what Ellen's new job was? Jessica was so concerned about herself that she didn't seem to understand a lot of what was going on around her. She would probably drop her new friend and Franny the minute she realized Ellen's position. The officers' ladies didn't associate with laundresses.

His heart lightened and he frowned. Was he glad about that? He was chagrined to discover he was jealous of Franny's attachment to Jessica. He shook his head and resolved to be glad for any pleasure his two precious cousins could find in Jessica's company. Some man of God he was. His attitude reminded him of Jonah's reluctance to go to the people of Nineveh. He didn't intend for the Lord to have to punish him for his lack of obedience.

Ellen came to the door when he knocked. She was dressed in an old cotton dress, and her hair was done up in a kerchief. She opened the door wide and gave him a welcoming smile. "Did you bring me some laundry?"

"I don't want to add to your work."

She chuckled. "And here I thought you'd be my first customer."

"Where's Franny?"

"Jessica came and took her for a walk."

He raised an eyebrow. "Has she figured out what your duties

are yet? I'm not so sure she'll associate with you when she knows you're a laundress."

"Clay, she's not as bad as you think. She seems to genuinely care about Franny, and she's been a friend to me. In fact, I think I'm the first real friend she's had."

He fell silent. For all his high resolve earlier, he was certainly failing already. "Can I help you with anything?"

She shook her head. "I have my fire blazing and my pot of water set over it. It's about hot enough. Several men have already dropped off their laundry, and I'm about to get started. It helps having Franny out from underfoot. My biggest fear is that she will get burned by the boiling water."

"I've worried about that too. I'll try to take her with me some when I'm here." He turned back toward the door. "Guess I'll let you get to work. I want a chance to talk to some of the men."

"When are you heading down to Colorado?"

"Not for a couple of weeks. I want to hold some services here first."

"Wonderful! Franny will be thrilled too." She waved and shut the door behind him.

The weak sunshine felt good on his arms as he strolled through the fort talking to the men. He held the reins for the blacksmith, Winston Claver, while he shod a skittish black stallion, and Clay helped some privates stack wood outside the sutler's store. The men were always surprised that a preacher would put his back into physical labor, but after he proved himself to them, they would usually at least listen when he talked about God.

He caught a glimpse of Jessica once or twice as she and Franny strolled about the fort under a pink lace parasol. He had to admit they made a pretty picture. Jessica had on a green dress and bonnet, and she had fixed Franny's hair just like hers. It had been all he could do to stop himself from rushing to take the child away from her. Would she ignore Franny when she realized she wasn't a little doll to dress up?

Jessica held Franny's hand and swung it as they walked along the path. She felt happy and content for some reason. Franny was a darling, and she was glad to be able to help Ellen. Jessica had been appalled when she realized what Ellen's job was, but she was beginning to get used to the idea now. She looked at her own soft, white hands and couldn't imagine doing something like that herself. Ellen's skin would be chapped and red by the time the day was over.

At lunchtime, she and Franny walked back to the DuBois quarters. "Mama, we're home." She found her mother in the kitchen preparing lunch.

Mama smiled. "I was just about to send Caleb out looking for you. Would you mind setting the table?"

Jessica looked at her sharply. Her mother had never before asked her to do any physical labor. She thought about protesting, but then she saw the weary strain on her mother's face. With reluctance Jessica went to the table, feeling strange as she laid out the plates and forks. The last time she'd done this she was eight years old, still living in the shanty by the river. She didn't like the feelings or the memories the small task aroused.

Where was Jasper now? She would likely never know.

"Why doesn't Uncle Samuel employ a striker to help you?" Most officers employed enlisted men to help with the housework and cooking. Her mother had always had some kind of help. Resentment burned when Jessica realized how much work her mother had been doing the past few days without any servants. Did Uncle Samuel intend to turn her into a drudge?

"I want to earn our keep." Mama pushed a stray strand of brown hair out of her eyes with the back of her hand. "Samuel already has a large household to support. I don't want to add to his burden. It was good of him to offer us a home. Besides, if Charlotte could do it, so can I."

Jessica compressed her lips. She was in too good a mood to fight with her mother, so she struggled to keep from blurting out what she thought about her new stepfather. If he was already making her mother compare herself with his first wife, it didn't bode well for the future of the marriage. And how could one compare the love of a first marriage with a marriage of convenience? It seemed so unfair.

"Where are the cousins?"

"Miriam went to pick up some vegetables for me at the sutler's store, Bridie is in her room, and Caleb is at the stables. They should all be here for lunch any minute." Her mother gave her a tired smile. "Don't look so glum, dear. I know it's an adjustment right now, but we'll soon feel a part of the family. Now, why don't you set this pretty little girl in a chair and give her some lunch?"

After the meal, Jessica walked back across the parade ground with Franny. The stink of lye stung her eyes as they neared Suds Row. She found Ellen bending over a steaming pot of clothing, her red face streaming with perspiration while her hair fell onto her shoulders in damp strands. She plunged her hands, red and raw from the soap, into the steaming heap of laundry and rubbed a shirt against the washboard.

Jessica winced just watching her. How could Ellen do it? Jessica couldn't do such a menial task if her life depended on it. "Are you almost done?"

Ellen straightened with a hand to her back and a heavy exhale. "Almost. Maybe another hour's work before I can quit for the day." She held out a chapped, red hand to Franny. "How's my girl? Did you enjoy your day with Jessica?"

Franny nodded and ran to cling to her mother's leg. "Jessie buyed me a licorice stick, and one of the soldiers whistled at us."

Jessica's face grew hot, and she dropped her gaze. She thought the child hadn't heard the whistle. She shuffled her feet. How could she have exposed little Franny to something like that? And she'd done it deliberately, now that she thought of it. She batted her lashes at the officers and smiled her best smile. Why did she feel such a need for approval from men? She was repeating what she'd seen her mother do in the shanty all those years. Man after man came through the battered door. She bit her lip and forced the thoughts away.

The little girl preened. "Jessie fixed my hair just like hers."

"I see that. You look like twins." Her mother's lips twitched with suppressed amusement as she turned to Jessica. "Thanks so much for spending the day with Franny. She already loves you."

A lump squeezed Jessica's throat. "I'll pick her up in the morning again. I enjoy having her around." She stayed and chatted a few moments, but Ellen seemed distracted by the laundry still piled beside her tub. With a final promise to call for Franny tomorrow, she waved good-bye and set off for home.

Jessica felt like skipping as she walked away from the little cabin. She actually had a friend. It felt so strange. Why had she never had a friend before? Trust was hard for her, but for some reason, Ellen made it easy. Jessica had always thought if she had a friend it would be someone beautiful, but Ellen was plain and plump. Her beauty was all on the inside.

Jessica rounded the corner of the sutler's store and was almost knocked over by Clay.

"Whoa!" He reached out to steady her.

When his hand touched her, a peculiar tingle went up her arm. Her mouth went dry, and her heart skipped a beat. She'd never felt anything like it. Was she getting sick? She drew back from Clay a bit and looked up at him.

"Sorry. I didn't look where I was going." He settled his Stetson on his head a bit more securely and turned in the direction she was heading. "I'll walk you to your quarters."

Jessica gave him a sidelong glance. Was he beginning to be interested? Why else would he offer to walk her home? "I'd like that," she said with the smile that usually fetched men from miles away.

But he showed no sign of being fetched. He casually took her hand and tucked it into the crook of his arm as he escorted her across the parade ground. Her hand felt warm and she flushed. What on earth was wrong with her?

"Did Franny give you any trouble?"

"Hardly. She was a perfect little angel all day." She could feel the muscles in his arm move as they strolled toward Officers' Row. Why was her mouth so dry? Her heart pounded like a Sioux drum too. Was she flushed with a fever maybe?

"I really appreciate your taking time with her. It's been so hard for her to lose her daddy. They were very close."

"She doesn't talk about him very much. What was he like?" She didn't really want to know, but she wanted to keep him with her a bit longer. They were almost to the porch of the DuBois quarters.

"Martin was a great guy. He would give his last dime to you if you needed it. He and I were more like brothers than cousins. When we were kids, I was always the daredevil, and he was the levelheaded one. He kept me out of more trouble. He joined up when I did, and when we were stationed out West, he told my mama he'd take care of me. I never expected that he would be called home before me."

Jessica felt uncomfortable at the indirect mention of religion. She could hardly believe that the strong, virile man beside her was a preacher. Personally, she avoided the thought of God as much as she could. He was just a vague being out there in the heavens somewhere, waiting to smash you like a bug if you got out of line. And she'd never been one for being told what to do.

They reached the steps to the porch, and Clay paused. Jessica slipped her hand from his elbow and started up the steps. She turned back a moment and gave him her best smile. "Thank you for escorting me. I'm taking Franny on a picnic tomorrow. Would you like to join us?"

Clay hesitated a moment, then nodded. "I haven't seen Franny much in the last few days. What time?"

"About eleven."

"Why don't you invite your cousins? I haven't gotten a chance to get to know them very well yet."

Jessica's smile faltered and heat rose in her cheeks. "Are you interested in Miriam?" She might as well learn what her obstacles were right now.

Clay chuckled. "I don't even know her. I just thought it would be a good time to get acquainted with all of them. Your mama too."

"That's not an answer." Jessica could hear the outrage in her voice, and she softened her tone. She didn't want him to think his answer was actually important to her. "You won't think much of Miriam when you get to know her. She's a spoiled child."

"Kind of like her cousin?" Clay's voice was amused.

"A little judgmental for a preacher, aren't we? Maybe I'll change your opinion of me." She gave him a slow smile, showing her dimple deliberately, then opened the door.

"You can begin by making an effort to be part of your new family," he called after her. "They'd probably love a picnic."

She just shrugged and shut the door behind her. She didn't want him to see how his words had wounded her. How dare he sit in judgment on her? He didn't know what it was like to be thrust into a family with no warning, to be made to feel like an unwelcome guest. She sniffed back tears of outrage and stalked down the hall to her bedroom.

Thankfully her cousins weren't in the room. She flung herself across her bed and buried her hot face in her down pillow. Clay deserved every bit of the humiliation coming his way. She'd show him he wasn't immune to beauty.

After supper her cousins cleared the table while she enjoyed a final cup of coffee. Uncle Samuel frowned when he saw her still seated at the table. She ignored his scowl and took another sip of coffee. She didn't know what was bothering him now, but she didn't care.

He cleared his throat. "I've tried to give you some space, Jessica, but I think it's time we laid down some rules around here."

"Rules?" Jessica didn't like the sound of that. She'd never had any rules, and she wasn't about to let this red-faced man in front of her give her any now.

"It has been pointed out to me that you never help with the dishes or the housework. You need to carry your share of the load and not leave it all for your mother and sisters. From now on, you three girls will take turns clearing and washing the supper dishes while your mother rests."

Jessica clenched her hands in her lap. "If you want to spare my mother some work, you can hire a striker like most caring husbands. You may have managed to get my mother as a drudge, but I will not be one for you. Or any man." She stood regally to her feet. "You are not my father. Your daughters are not my sisters, and I will not be told what to do." She gathered her skirts in one hand and started from the room.

"Stop!" he thundered. "I will not be spoken to this way in my own house! You will do as you are told, or you will leave my home and protection."

Beyond his angry glare Jessica could see the pale oval of her mother's distressed face, but nothing could stop her white-hot rage now. "Nothing would please me more!" she spat. "I didn't want to come here in the first place. Feel free to send me back to Boston." She gave him a final contemptuous look, then went to her room.

Even with the door shut, she could hear his raised voice in the kitchen and her mother's soft, pleading tones. The nerve of the man. Did he think he could order her around when her own father had never so much as raised his voice to her? She paced the room and thought about all the other things she should have said.

After a few minutes she sighed and sat on the faded quilt that covered the bed. Truth be told, she really wasn't all that eager to go back to Boston just yet. She was enjoying her friendship with Ellen and her pursuit of Clay. Not that she was making much headway with him, but the chase was enjoyable. She couldn't let her uncle tell her what to do, though. The angry voices had stilled in the kitchen, but she could still hear soft murmurs.

She picked up a book of Miriam's and leafed through it. It was a wild tale about Indians–did her uncle know his daughter read trashy dime novels?–but at least if someone came in the room, they would see she was so unconcerned about the confrontation in the kitchen that she was reading instead of worrying.

After a few moments someone tapped on the door. "Jessica, may I come in?" Her mother's voice was fraught with tension.

"Of course, Mama." Jessica put the book down beside her and folded her hands in her lap.

Her mother stepped into the room and closed the door. She stood looking at Jessica, then cleared her throat. "Darling, surely you must see that everyone must help out just a bit. Couldn't you agree to at least help clear away the supper dishes twice a week? It would only take you a few minutes. I told Samuel that I really couldn't condone forcing you to do dishes, but he insists you must do something."

"And what will he do if I don't?"

Her mother fluttered her hands helplessly. "He will turn you out."

"Oh, really?" Jessica gave a short, mirthless laugh. "Just turn me out into the street? I think the commanding officer would have something to say about that." She knew that would terrify her uncle. The colonel was enamored with her.

Her mother's white face paled even more. "You wouldn't speak to Colonel Edwards? Samuel wouldn't like that at all."

"Well, then you tell dear Uncle Samuel that I will do no more than help you set the table for supper. Otherwise, I will have to speak to Colonel Edwards about this situation." She felt sorry for her mother's distress, but Jessica would hold to her guns now.

Maybe, though, she could help her mother in small ways without Uncle Samuel finding out.

"Of course, dear. You've been doing that anyway. I'll tell your uncle." She fluttered her hands again and hurried from the room.

Jessica let out a sigh of relief. She'd won that skirmish. For now. But if she knew her uncle, and she was beginning to, it wasn't the end of the war. With Miriam keeping him stirred up, the next battle wouldn't be far away.

She thought about Clay's request for her to invite her cousins on their picnic tomorrow. Maybe she could work out some kind of truce with Miriam if she made the effort. The very thought made her grit her teeth, but she had to do something.

At least she wasn't going back to Boston just yet. She pushed away the image of Clay's handsome face. Her desire to stay at Fort Bridger had nothing to do with him, not really.

Four

By the time boots and saddles, the morning bugle call for the cavalry to mount their horses, rang out, Clay was already dressed and striding toward the stables. But first he wanted to stop in and see how Ellen's first day had gone. The lantern glowed softly from her quarters, and he bounded up the front steps.

She opened the door and smiled. "I'm fine. You worry too much."

"Someone has to worry about you. You don't worry about yourself." Clay shut the door behind him and followed her to the kitchen table. The laundress quarters were modest by any standards: a tiny one-room cabin furnished with a crude wooden table, a small bed she shared with Franny, and a battered bench. A small fire burned in the fireplace, scenting the air with pine. A tuft of Franny's blonde hair peeked out of the bedcovers, and he felt a pang of remorse that he hadn't been able to do better for them. These quarters were much sparser than what they had been used to as the dependents of an army officer. When he'd asked the post commander for the job for Ellen, Colonel Edwards had been astonished that anyone would request such a menial job for a relative.

"Coffee?" She held up the coffeepot.

"Sure."

She poured the coffee into a cracked cup. "You had breakfast?"

"Probably before you were out of bed." He took a gulp of hot coffee. "You ready to quit yet? There'll be a stage through here tomorrow heading east."

Ellen smiled gently. "You know better than that. It's hard work, but I'll get used to it. And once I get enough money put by, we'll find a small house in a safe town and move on."

"I hear Jessica is taking Franny on a picnic today."

She nodded. "I don't know how I'd ever do this job without Jessica. It is such a blessing not to have to look after Franny or worry about her being scorched by the laundry water. I think you've misjudged our friend. She really is a sweetheart."

Clay snorted. "Sweet is not how I would describe her. More like hard and calculating."

Ellen lifted her eyebrows. "I've never known you to take such an immediate dislike to someone before. Her selfish attitude is just a wall of protection. You should get to know her better."

Clay flushed at the gentle reprimand. What was it about Jessica? Ellen was right. It was odd for him to be so antagonistic to someone. Where were all of his lofty intentions from yesterday? How could he show her God's love when he couldn't even bring himself to say a nice word about the woman? "I'm going on the picnic with them today."

Ellen brightened. "Wonderful! Franny will have her two favorite people in the world dancing attendance on her."

He laughed. "When do you suppose her highness will wake up?"

"Anytime now. I'm surprised she's still sleeping. Probably all the excitement from yesterday. And she hasn't been sleeping well since Martin died. She still cries out for him in the night."

Clay grimaced. He had wanted to make up for the loss of her father, but he'd been foolish to think his presence could remove that pain.

Ellen touched his hand. "Don't worry, Clay. We'll be fine eventually. We just have to get through one day at a time. God's provision has been wonderful." She dropped her hand and turned away. "Now why don't you wake her up? I need to get her dressed anyway. I'll have to get started on my work soon."

Clay walked to the bed and nudged her shoulder. With her pink cheeks and tousled blonde hair, she was a beautiful sight. His eyes misted as he remembered the day she was born. Martin had been so proud and happy, but now he would never watch his darling little girl grow to womanhood. Clay vowed to do better to help and protect her. After all, he doubted he would ever have any children of his own. What woman would ever want to take second place to his calling?

By the time Ellen had dressed Franny, Jessica called from the front porch. When Ellen opened the front door, Clay caught his breath at Jessica's beauty. Her blue gown emphasized her eyes, and the way she'd tied her curls back in a bow revealed the perfection of her face.

What was he thinking? He didn't have any use for beautiful women. They never had any thoughts beyond their looks and what they wanted. This woman was certainly no exception.

Jessica stepped into the room. "Is Franny ready?"

"I'll get her," Ellen said. "You'll never know how much it means to me for you to take time with her."

Jessica smiled up at Clay while Ellen left to get Franny. "I've decided to take on Franny's education."

"Oh?" He crossed his arms over his chest. "Bored?"

She flushed. "Don't you think Franny needs an education? When would Ellen have time with all her work?"

"Sure, but so do the other children in camp. You could start a school for all of them."

Her color deepened. "Why do you persist in baiting me? I thought we were going to have a nice picnic and enjoy the day."

Clay shuffled his feet. He had to watch his tongue if he had any chance of winning her to the Lord. "You're right. I'm sorry."

She lifted her eyebrows at his apology, then smiled sweetly. "You're forgiven. Where would be a good place to go for lunch? I'm going to start lessons with Franny until eleven or so, then we can meet for our picnic."

"There's a grassy knoll overlooking the river just a half mile from the fort. I'll pick you up at eleven. Will you be at your house?"

Jessica nodded, then tilted her head to look up at him. "I did what you asked."

Clay frowned. What had he asked her?

"I invited my cousins on the picnic."

Clay managed to hide his surprise. "Now that wasn't too painful, was it?"

She tossed her red curls. "Of course not. They were delighted to accept. But don't say I didn't warn you. Miriam will probably spend the afternoon flirting outrageously with you. Bridie will have her nose stuck in a book, and Caleb will pester you with questions about Indians."

Clay grinned. "I think I can handle it." He gave her a wave and went to make his visits with a couple of ill soldiers. He had to admit he was surprised she'd actually followed his suggestion. It must suit her schemes somehow. Jessica seemed to be a woman who knew exactly what she wanted and how to get it.

By the time Jessica got back to her home, she had managed to stop seething. Clay Cole really was a most infuriating man. Not even a word of appreciation that she'd done as he asked. But she was determined to get through that indifferent shell of his somehow.

She took Franny to the bedroom and sat her down at a small table with a primer she'd found in her mother's trunk. The morning passed quickly, and by eleven Franny had begun to recognize some of her letters.

Jessica closed the book and went to change her clothes. She dressed carefully in a sky-blue dress lavished with cream lace and tied her hair back with cream lace that matched the dress. She pinched her cheeks to redden them and wet her lips. Turning this way and that in the mirror, she didn't see how Clay would be able to resist her. She turned at a knock on the door.

"Jessica, dear, that lovely Reverend Cole is here for your picnic. The rest of the children are in the kitchen waiting."

"We're coming." She took Franny's hand and followed her mother to the kitchen, where Miriam stood laughing close to Clay's face. Jessica's stomach clenched. She didn't care what he did or who he flirted with.

Franny flung herself against Clay's legs.

"Hey, muffin." He scooped her into his arms and hugged her. "Are you ready for a picnic?"

She nodded vigorously. "Jessie teached me my letters." She puffed out her chest. "I'm gonna learn to write my name and read."

Clay looked suitably impressed. "I didn't learn to read until I was five, and you won't even be four until next month."

She preened, then slid down to the floor and ran to Jessica and hugged her skirts. "Jessie is my friend."

A warm glow filled her. "Are we ready to go?" She stroked Franny's silken hair.

"I brought the fishing poles."

Fishing poles? Jessica frowned at Clay. She'd never been fishing in her life, and the thought didn't appeal to her now.

Miriam clapped. "I love fishing!"

She couldn't let her cousin best her. She shrugged. "Then fishing it is." She was desperate to think of a reason to stay home. This was not the day she'd planned.

"I packed you some boiled eggs and potato salad," her mother said. "I'll put in a skillet and lard to fry up the fish you catch."

Jessica suppressed a shudder at the thought of frying fish,

though she supposed she could do it if she had to. She'd watched her mother often enough, but she hated the way frying fish made her hair smell. Would she be expected to clean the fish too?

Mama handed Caleb the lunch basket, and they all filed out the door to the waiting two-seat wagon. Clay tossed the gear in the back, then helped Miriam onto the front seat. Caleb climbed up to sit in the back. He lifted Jessica, Franny, and Bridie into the back before he swung up beside Miriam.

Jessica ground her teeth as her cousin flirted with Clay all the way to the river. Meanwhile Bridie kept up a steady stream of questions, and Jessica found it hard to keep from snapping at her. Why had she ever let herself be talked into inviting her cousins? They were just in the way. They were never going to be a family.

When Clay stopped the wagon, the fort was only a blur in the distance. Blackbirds circled overhead, and the air smelled fresh and moist from the Black River gurgling its way down the mountain. Small, puffy clouds drifted lazily across the blue sky.

In the shade of a large tree along the riverbank, Clay tethered the horses and lifted the ladies down from the wagon. "Find us a likely fishing hole, Caleb. I'm starved."

While Caleb scrambled to do as he was asked, Clay spread the blankets under the protective canopy of the trees, then handed the fishing poles to Jessica. "Why don't you get these baited?"

Baited? Trying to hide her dismay, Jessica took the poles and the can of bait from him. She thought about refusing, but the challenge in his eyes stopped her. She eyed the sharp and dangerous-looking fishhook, then handed the bait can to Franny, and they carried them over to the riverbank. Miriam stayed with Clay, but Bridie followed Jessica.

"Over here!" Caleb waved to her from farther down the river.

With reluctance she led the way to where Caleb stood peering into the clear water. She laid the fishing poles on a rock and took the bait can from Franny. "Um, Caleb, would you like to bait the poles?"

"Pa says everyone should bait his own hook. Here, I'll show you." He grabbed the can and opened it. He rummaged around in it for a moment, then extracted a large, squirming worm. A night crawler, she remembered her brother calling them. Caleb poked the sharp hook into the worm's body in several places and tossed it into the river. "Nothing to it."

Jessica felt nauseated at the disgusting action. Bridie took a worm and threaded it on the hook the same way Caleb had done.

"I can do it." Franny jumped up and down. "My daddy showed me how." She dug her small fingers into the can and drew out a worm.

"Be careful with the hook."

Franny nodded at Jessica. "Daddy told me." She took a few moments longer than the other two, but she managed to get the worm on the hook. She looked at Jessica expectantly.

Jessica fought the panic rising in her throat. She just couldn't touch a worm. Maybe she could get Franny to do it for her when no one was looking . . . She jumped when she heard Clay's deep voice behind her.

"Ready?" He stepped closer, and she shivered at his warm

breath on her neck. She didn't understand these strange sensations she felt whenever she was close to him, but she didn't like them. She pushed away the shivery feeling and turned to face him. She would just tell him she couldn't touch a worm. But when she saw the amused look on his face, the words died in her throat.

Miriam was only steps behind him. She took a fishing pole and a worm and went to sit on a warm rock. Her hook and worm went into the river with a gentle splash, and she rinsed her fingers off in the water.

Jessica looked at Clay, then down at the pole and bait can. She had to do it. Somehow she just had to do it. She swallowed the bile in her throat. "Take yours, then I'll go on downriver."

With a knowing look Clay took a pole, pulled a worm from the can, and walked over to a nearby rock. Jessica stared at his broad back as she picked up the last pole. She took the bait can and walked a bit downstream from the others. Glancing behind her to make sure no one was watching, she shook the worm out of the can and onto the warm rock. She nearly screamed when she saw the fat, wriggling body. She bit her lip until she tasted blood, then took her hook with determination. Holding the hook firmly between her thumb and index finger, she stabbed the barbed end into the middle of the worm's body. The cold flesh of the worm touched her finger, and she dropped the hook with a soft moan.

"Need some help?"

She stood up quickly at Clay's voice. "Not at all. I'm ready to start fishing." She flung the hook and worm into the water before Clay could see how poorly the worm was attached. She should have poked the hook through in another spot, but she could not touch that cold body again.

"I'll fish here beside you for a while," he said. "Franny is with Bridie."

Jessica nearly groaned. His presence was the last thing she needed. She didn't want him to realize she'd never been fishing before. She glanced upriver to make sure Franny was doing all right, then eased down on the rock and stared at the bobber floating in the water. How was she supposed to know when she got a stupid fish anyway? She felt Clay sit beside her, but she didn't look at him. He would surely be able to read her expression.

After about five minutes she felt a tug on the pole, and the bobber ducked under the water. Was the worm trying to escape? What would she do if it did? She just couldn't put another worm on that hook. The bobber jerked again and stayed under the surface.

Clay jumped to his feet. "Hey, are you sleeping? You've got a bite!"

A bite? Did that mean the fish had teeth? She shuddered at the thought just as the pole jerked again and almost went flying out of her hands. She stood and gingerly pulled on the fishing pole. The fish pulled back. She scowled and jerked up on the pole. A large trout, dripping and wriggling, flew straight for her head. She shrieked and swung the pole to the left. Before Clay could react, the wet fish slapped him in the face. He shoved it away, and Jessica swung the pole again.

"Watch out!"

This time it landed in his armpit. He jumped away, but she

threw the pole and fish into the sand at his feet. "Why didn't you stay out of my way?" She dared a glance at him. A single fish scale clung to the tip of his nose and shimmered in the sunlight.

Clay brushed at the sand and water on his face. "I didn't know fishing with you would be dangerous. What were you trying to do–behead me?"

Jessica drew herself up to her full five feet four inches. "I was doing just fine until you came over here breathing down my neck. Why don't you go stare at Miriam? She would welcome your attentions, but I do not."

Clay's lips twitched, and he made a strange sound. Was he laughing at her? She glared at him.

He choked again, then roared with laughter. "Red, you should see your face! You've never had a fishing pole in your hand before, have you?"

"Don't call me Red. I hate that name!" She chose to ignore his question about her fishing experience.

"What's wrong with Red? It suits you. In fact, I think I'll call you that from now on." Clay grinned again.

She stamped her foot and turned to storm away.

"Hey, Red."

She whirled, but Clay interrupted before she could say anything.

"You forgot your fish. You'll want to clean it and get it ready to cook."

Clean it? She didn't have any idea how to do that. She shuffled back to the fish and looked down at it. She looked back up into Clay's expectant face, then tipped up her chin. "I'm not in the mood for fish."

"Well, I am. That's a nice trout you caught. We can't waste it. Besides, I should have something for my trials. I've never had a cold, wet fish in my armpit before, and I can't say as I recommend the experience." He knelt and removed the fish from the hook with a practiced jerk, then stood and held it out to her. "Here you go. But pardon me if I don't stand too close while you have the knife in your hand."

She managed a feeble smile as she reached out an unsteady hand to gingerly take the fish by the tail. The cold, slimy feel of it raised a bubble of nausea in her throat, and she couldn't look in its staring eye. With it held out in front of her, she walked over to the rock where Clay had laid out his fillet knife and some newspaper. She put the fish on the paper and picked up the knife. What did she do next?

"Hey, you need some help?" Caleb's hair stood up in spikes where he'd swiped a wet hand through it, and he carried a string of four fish.

Jessica had never seen a more welcome sight than his eager smile. He wasn't making fun of her and actually seemed to want to help. "Don't tell anyone, but I've never cleaned fish before."

His grin widened. "You think we don't know that? It's nothing to be chicken about. I'll show you." He took the knife from her unresisting fingers and proceeded to scrape the scales off all five fish, then showed her how to gut and fillet them.

Jessica didn't really want to watch, but it was the least she could do. In spite of the mess, she found herself actually interested in the deft way he handled the knife and how quickly he prepared the fish for cooking.

When he was done, he handed the fillets to her. "I get the biggest piece."

"You can have two." She narrowed her eyes. "Why did you help me? I haven't been exactly warm to you."

Caleb hesitated. "Last Sunday at church Clay told us to do something nice for someone you don't much cotton to, so I picked you. But you know what? You're not so bad. When you first came here, you were like a bear with a sore head, always snarlin' and uppity. But once I saw you don't know everything, you were okay. I guess I could stand having another sister." He blushed bright red and ducked his head.

He left Jessica with her mouth open. The heat rose in her face, but whether it was from pleasure because he liked her or because of how he had seen her before today, she wasn't really sure. She looked down at the fish fillets in her hand and smiled. At least she knew how to cook them, even if she hated doing it.

Clay had made a fire beside the water and stacked some rocks as a ledge for the skillet to rest on. As she cooked the fish, she thought about what Caleb had said. Was that really how people saw her? Cross and uppity? She wanted to be thought of as a force to be reckoned with, but not as someone who snarled at people and was totally unapproachable. She'd always wanted people to see her as beautiful and cultured but likable.

Clay thought she was frivolous, without any real purpose in life. What *was* her purpose in life? What could fill this void, this insatiable hunger inside her? Her eyes smarted, and she tried to tell herself it was from the smoke of the fire, but deep inside she knew better. She wasn't happy, and she had never really been settled and content with herself or her life. She was good at putting on a facade, a beautiful and smiling face to fool everyone. But now it seemed no one had been fooled after all. No one at all.

Five

For several days after the picnic, Jessica kept pretty much to herself. She began to notice how the others tiptoed around her as if afraid of incurring her wrath. Was that what she wanted? To be feared? As she watched her cousins interact with their father and her mother, she often felt like an outsider. She had never had that kind of loving relationship with anyone, not even with her biological mother. She'd never felt she was a real, necessary part of a whole. Even her doting parents had seemed to stand together as a unit, loving her as a separate entity. She didn't know how to go about becoming part of a family.

Morose, she wandered over to talk to Ellen about her feelings. She'd never really bared her soul to anyone before, but maybe it was time.

Ellen had just put Franny to bed. The little girl sat up with a delighted smile when Jessica came into the cabin. "Jessie!" She reached out her arms. "Will you tell me a story?"

Now what? She didn't know any stories, but she stepped to the side of the bed and sat down. "What kind of story?"

Franny seemed lost in thought for a moment. "How about one with a little girl with red hair like yours?" She reached up and touched one of Jessica's curls.

"Well . . . once upon a time there was a little girl named Ruth. She had red hair but she hated it."

"Oh no, Jessie, she couldn't hate it."

Jessica tickled her. "Am I telling the story or are you?"

Franny squealed and giggled. "You are, you are. But any little girl would want hair like yours."

Jessica smiled. "This little girl didn't. She hated her hair. She wanted beautiful blonde hair like her friend Alice. Anyway, Ruth lived in a tiny house with her younger brother, Jasper, and her mother, Mary. It was dirty and there were bugs, but they had each other."

"What about her daddy?"

"Her daddy, uh, he ran–I mean, he didn't live there anymore. He went out west to find some land for his family and was gone a long time. Anyway, Jasper had a tadpole he'd caught in the creek behind the house, and my, how he loved that tadpole. Ruth did too. One day she decided to surprise Jasper and find him another tadpole to keep the first one company. She took off her shoes and socks and waded in the creek with an old tin cup, trying to find a tadpole. She stepped into a hole in the creek and got all muddy. But she found that tadpole. She was so happy when she walked home because she just knew Jasper was going to be happy to have another tadpole. When she got home and her mother saw how muddy she was, she was sent to bed without supper."

"How mean," Franny said with a pout. "You would never do that to me, would you, Mommy?"

Ellen shook her head. She looked as engrossed in the story as her daughter.

Jessica smiled at Ellen. "Well, your mommy is a special kind of mommy. But back to the story. Ruth went along to the little room she shared with Jasper. She didn't care about supper, since she got the tadpole. She hurried to the jar where his tadpole was, and guess what she found?"

"What?" Franny asked breathlessly.

"There was a *frog* in the jar. It was trying to keep its head above water and looking kind of sickly. Ruth was shocked. Where had the frog come from? She got it out of the jar before it could drown, then looked all over for the tadpole. She couldn't find it anywhere, so she figured the frog somehow got in the jar and ate the tadpole.

"She put her new tadpole in the jar and screwed the lid on tight so the frog couldn't get back in and eat it. Just then Jasper came home. When she told him what had happened, he laughed at her and told her that the frog used to be the tadpole but had grown up and changed."

"Really? It really changed?"

"It sure did. Ruth was surprised too. But the more she thought about it, the more excited she got. Because that meant that maybe she could change too. Maybe she was just a tadpole now, but someday she could be somebody special. And she decided she *would* be someone special."

Franny frowned when Jessica fell silent. "That's not the end of the story, is it?"

Jessica laughed. "It is for tonight. I'll finish it some other time." She tucked the covers around Franny and kissed her on the nose. "Now you go to sleep, little tadpole, and dream about what kind of frog you want to be when you grow up."

"I want to be just like you," Franny murmured sleepily. She snuggled down into the covers and closed her eyes.

Just like her. The words rang in her ears. Was she any kind of person a little girl should emulate? She was afraid she wouldn't like the honest answer to that question.

"Would you like some tea?" Ellen asked.

"That sounds wonderful." She was glad for the interruption of her thoughts. She followed Ellen to the kitchen table and sat down while her friend put the kettle on to boil. She leaned her chin into her hand and watched Ellen's quick movements. Where did she get all her energy? Surely she must be exhausted from doing laundry all day.

Ellen sat in a chair and gave her a penetrating look. "That story sounded true. Was it?"

Jessica curved her mouth in a slight smile. "Yes. That really happened."

"Who was Ruth? A friend?"

Sudden tears welled up in her eyes. What was wrong with her lately? She *never* cried. "No, it was me."

Ellen looked at her sharply. "You had a brother? Letty never mentioned it."

Jessica felt tongue-tied for a moment. "I was adopted." She had never told anyone outside the family the story. "My father went off out west and never came back. My mother took up with different men until she was killed when I was eight. The police came and took me and Jasper. Several weeks later I was adopted by Mama and Papa DuBois."

Ellen was silent for a moment, but her eyes were wet. "What happened to Jasper?"

Tears spilled down Jessica's cheeks, and she scrubbed at them furiously. "I don't know. I never saw him again." The constant pain had been with her all these years. She just wished she knew Jasper was okay.

"Oh, my dear Jessica, I'm so sorry you had to go through such pain, especially at such a young age. Life can be hard. But you can thank God that he put you into such a warm and loving family."

"But I'm not happy. I know I should be. I have everything a woman could want. What's wrong with me?" The cry came from her heart. Was this all there was to life? Her lips trembled and she swallowed hard.

Ellen took her hand. "Happiness is something different from real joy and peace. God gives us joy and peace through good times and bad. He's what keeps us stable through whatever life throws our way."

Jessica shook her head. "Where was God when my family was ripped apart? Where was God when Papa died? God doesn't care about me now. He never has."

"Oh, you're so wrong, Jessie. God has always loved you. He's there for you if you will just turn to him and ask for his help."

"What do you mean? If he's there, why should I have to ask?" Jessica drew her hand out of Ellen's grasp. She had never begged in her life, and she wasn't about to start now.

"God never forces his presence on his children. How would you like it if your mother was always butting in and telling you how to do things and never letting you learn anything on your own? God wants to be your comfort and your strength. But you have to come to the end of yourself, where you realize you are helpless and that the only way to heaven and God's peace is by what Jesus did on the cross for you. He took your punishment for everything you've done wrong in your life. He reconciled you to God–but you have to receive his free gift of grace."

Jessica shook her head again. It made no sense to her. But she did envy Ellen's peace and contentment. Even through her bereavement, she had been strong and somehow secure.

"I can see you don't understand. Why don't you come to church with me and Franny on Sunday? Clay explains it so well."

Clay. Just the mention of his name set her heart to pounding. "What do you think Clay really thinks of me?"

Ellen was silent for a moment, and Jessica could read the answer on her face. "He thinks I'm a frivolous, spoiled brat, doesn't he?"

"He doesn't know you as well as I do." She touched Jessica's hand again. "But he'll see who you really are someday."

Jessica twisted her mouth into a wry smile. "Maybe a vain, selfish woman is all I am, Ellen. Maybe you're the one who will see the real me someday." She stood and stretched. "I'd better get home and let you get to bed. Thanks for listening. I've never had a friend before. It's nice." She bent and kissed Ellen's cheek. "You're a peach."

The next morning when she went to pick up Franny, the day was warm and lovely. Spring was here in full bloom. When she saw wisps of thistledown floating in the wind, she realized that's all her life was: a bit of will-o'-the-wisp pulled in any direction the wind blew. But she didn't want to be like that. She wanted to have real purpose in life.

When Jessica knocked on the door, she could hear Franny's piping voice reciting her ABCs. She swallowed hard. Franny had remembered what she'd been taught so far, so that was at least one good thing Jessica had done in her life, if God was keeping score.

Ellen opened the door and her face crinkled into a smile. "It's about time you got here. Franny has been driving me crazy wondering where you were."

The room was pleasantly perfumed with smoke from the woodstove and toasting bread. Jessica felt a pang of wistfulness for the simple pleasures Ellen enjoyed with Franny. She had never felt the contentment that glowed on Ellen's face. That happiness seemed so elusive. Would she ever feel it herself? How did one go about finding it?

Franny looked up from her perch on Clay's lap. "Jessie!" Dimples flashing, she slid to the floor and hurtled toward Jessica.

Jessica knelt and held out her arms. "You're doing very well with your ABCs." She swept her up. The feel of that small, warm body brought moisture to her eyes. It was a strange feeling, one she wasn't sure she liked. It was safer not to get involved with other people, safer not to open herself up to pain and disappointment. But she'd already done it now.

Clay stood and thrust his hands in his pockets. "Run out of things to do?"

Jessica thrust her chin in the air. "Did you?"

He laughed. "Touché. Truce?" He held out his hand.

"Truce." She shook his hand and quickly let go when her heart for some strange reason began to race. The wisest thing would be to avoid him altogether, but she was determined not to let him get the upper hand in their relationship.

"Have you had breakfast?" Ellen cut fresh slices of bread and reached for the jam.

Jessica's stomach rumbled before she could answer.

"I guess that's a no." Ellen laughed. "That was a hungry stomach if I ever heard one."

"It does smell good," Jessica admitted. "But are you sure you have enough?"

"She means are you sure you have enough to feed a hungry man as well as the rest of you?" Clay put in. "Just to set your minds at ease, I had breakfast–but I wouldn't turn down a bit of toast."

Jessica carried Franny over to the table and sat in the chair beside Clay. She thought about asking if she could help Ellen, but she might ask Jessica to do something she didn't know how to do, and she didn't want to betray any more ignorance to Clay. Besides, since when was what a woman could *do* important? All that mattered was that she was beautiful and cultured–and on that basis, she was a success.

Jessica tilted her chin and straightened her shoulders, proud of her beauty and culture. No one had the right to mold her into something she wasn't. Just because Clay's mother had prejudiced him against beautiful women didn't mean she had to be ashamed of being beautiful.

They spent a pleasant breakfast laughing and talking about nothing and everything. She flirted with Clay, and although he showed no sign of responding, she enjoyed the challenge in his hazel eyes. She was careful to keep complacency from her expression, though. There was something about Clay. Something that made her want him to see beyond her outer beauty. Jessica wanted him to see what she saw in Ellen, that inner loveliness that seemed to emanate from within.

Clay was thoughtful as he walked away from Ellen's cabin. He didn't know what to make of Jessica. He had thought he knew just what kind of person she was from the moment he met her, but then she would do something that seemed so out of character. Like the challenge he'd given her to invite her cousins. He'd been shocked when she actually did it, and then she managed to make friends with Caleb. After lunch she had even laughed and talked with Miriam and Bridie. And he had thought she would soon lose interest in Franny, especially once she realized the officers' wives wouldn't associate with Ellen. But instead of being embarrassed to be associated with a laundress and her child, she faithfully took Franny for lessons every day and often dropped in after supper to visit with Ellen.

She had even come to some services at the fort. For some reason, though, her big blue eyes gazing at him all through the service had been distracting. There was no way he would let himself get involved with someone like Jessica DuBois. No woman would want to play second fiddle to God.

He spent the day working on his Sunday message, but Jessica's beautiful face kept intruding on his concentration. He finally threw down his pen in disgust and stretched. His two weeks at Fort Bridger were almost up, and it was time to think about moving on to Colorado. Maybe the day after tomorrow would be a good time to head out.

He made his plans and left two days later. Jessica had wished him a quiet good-bye, and he wondered what she was thinking. Sometimes she got a strange look in her eyes, and he wasn't sure what it meant. A haunted, hungry look full of pain and longing.

Most of the summer passed before he knew it. He alternated his time between three different forts, but he found himself looking forward to his visits at Fort Bridger. For one thing, the men there were beginning to respond to his message, and three of them had accepted Christ on his last visit. But if he was honest, he would have to admit that he looked forward most to the verbal sparring with Jessica. She was an intriguing woman, and he had to keep reminding himself to protect his emotions. The last thing he wanted was to develop any tender feelings for her. The man who fell into her clutches would rue the day.

In early September he arrived back at Fort Bridger, feeling restless and at odds with himself. He grabbed his jacket and strolled toward Ellen's cabin, but to his surprise she wasn't out beside her tub of laundry. The fire was out. Obviously she hadn't done any laundry today. He rapped his knuckles against the door and waited. After a few minutes he knocked again, then turned to go. Maybe she had taken Franny for a walk.

He'd taken only one step when the door creaked open behind him. Ellen leaned against the doorjamb. Alarm raced through him at the sight of her white face and labored breathing.

"Clay. Thank God," she whispered. "I've prayed and prayed for you to come."

In two quick steps he was at her side and caught her just as she staggered and nearly fell. "Ellen! Here, let me get you to bed."

The heat radiating off her body made his mouth go dry with dread. Sweat had plastered her hair to her head, and she smelled of dried sweat and vomit. How long had she been sick? He half carried, half dragged her to her bed. He glanced around for Franny, then found her asleep at the foot of the bed. She looked okay, and he breathed a sigh of relief that she'd been spared whatever illness had struck Ellen.

He laid Ellen on the bed and pulled a thin blanket over her. "I'll be right back with the doctor."

"Franny," Ellen whispered. "You must get Franny away from me."

"She's asleep right now. She'll be fine until I get back with the doctor."

"No! Get her out of here now!" Ellen pushed herself up and yanked on Clay's arm.

"Okay, okay." He eased her back against the pillow, then scooped Franny up. She didn't even awaken. "I'll take her with me. You rest and I'll be right back."

He hurried across the parade ground to the infirmary, almost colliding with Jessica as she and Bridie came out of the sutler's store. "Here." He handed Franny to Jessica. "Ellen's sick, and I've got to fetch the doctor."

Jessica's mouth opened, but Clay didn't wait for her questions. He barreled through the door to the infirmary, shouting for the doctor.

Doctor Harold Mason stood washing his hands at a table on the far side of the room, a tall, well-built man with dark hair. With a weary shrug, he turned to face Clay. "No need to make such a ruckus, Preacher. I'm not deaf."

"My cousin Ellen is real sick, Doc." The door opened behind him, and he caught a whiff of Jessica's familiar honeysuckle sachet. "You've got to come with me right now."

Doctor Mason sighed. "Cholera, most likely." He frowned. "It's spreading like wildfire."

Cholera. The very word struck terror to Clay's heart, and Jessica caught her breath behind him. Clay figured now she'd give Franny right back to him for fear of catching the disease herself. When he turned toward her, though, she handed Franny to Bridie.

"Take Franny home with you and tell Mama what's happened," she said in a firm, no-nonsense voice. "I've got to take care of Ellen."

Clay raised his eyebrows, but he was in no position to turn down her offer. Doctor Mason grabbed his bag and followed them out into the street. Clay led the way back to Suds Row.

When he entered the cabin this time, the strong odor of sickness hit him in the face. His gut churned as he hurried to the bed. Ellen lay on her side with her legs drawn up to her chest.

Doctor Mason pushed him out of the way. "Go fix some coffee or something, and let me look at her." He bent over Ellen's inert form and opened his bag.

Clay turned away and sank bonelessly into a chair. The feeling of dread grew, and he bowed his head and prayed fervently for Ellen. How could little Franny survive without her mother? Ellen *had* to pull through.

He sensed Jessica moving around him and opened his eyes to see what she was doing. Her face set in concentration, she was trying to make coffee. She frowned at the coffeepot, and he could tell she had never made coffee before. He stood and nudged her to one side. "Here, let me show you."

She didn't come back with her usual sharp comment but let him demonstrate what to do. "Thank you," she said softly. "I'll remember next time."

He was suddenly overwhelmed with gratitude for her presence. Her concern surprised him. He turned to see what the doctor was doing, but the man's bulky form blocked Ellen from view. Clay sat in the chair again and buried his face in his hands. Cholera was deadly. He'd had a good friend die from it back in '64. It took him fast too.

Doctor Mason cleared his throat, put his instruments in his bag, and walked to the table. "That coffee done yet? I haven't had a minute to even eat today. The first case of cholera showed up last night. It's sweeping through Fort Bridger like a herd of stampeding buffalo."

Jessica poured them all a cup of coffee and sat beside the doctor. "What do we need to do for Ellen?" She cut the doctor a slice of bread, buttered it, and spread it with jam.

Doctor Mason bit appreciatively into the jam and bread. He swallowed and sighed. "That does hit the spot." He shook his head. "It will just have to run its course. I gave her laudanum, but anything I do is like barkin' at a knot. Only thing you can do is give her plenty of fluids, keep her clean, and stay alert in case she chokes when she vomits."

Jessica nodded. "I can do that."

"I'll help too," Clay said.

The doctor finished his coffee and bread. "Send for me if you need me. There's not much any of us can do but pray, though. She'll either pull through on her own or she won't." He picked up his bag and headed for the door. "I have other patients to check on. I'll try to stop back later tonight."

When he shut the door behind him, Jessica stood. "I'll take the first watch. Why don't you go check on Franny while I get Ellen cleaned up. We need to make sure Franny doesn't get sick too."

Clay hesitated, but what she said made sense. He wasn't sure if he trusted her to care for Ellen by herself, but she should be the one to clean her up. And he was worried about Franny. He picked up his hat and jammed it on his head. "I'll be back in a little while." He stopped when he reached the door. "Why are you doing this?" He still found it hard to believe Jessica would risk her own health for Ellen.

"She's my friend. I've never had a friend before." She went to the little chest against the wall where spare clothing was kept. "Go check on Franny. I can handle getting Ellen cleaned up."

Clay shrugged and went outside. Letty met him at the door with soft words of concern. He told her what the doctor had said and that he and Jessica would be caring for Ellen. She promised to help in any way she could, then showed him into the bedroom where Franny lay sleeping. He touched her forehead, but she felt cool. Her color looked good, and she was breathing evenly. Satisfied that she wasn't getting sick, he closed the door softly and went across the parade ground to Ellen's cabin.

When he let himself in, Jessica was holding Ellen upright, trying to force some tea down her throat. Ellen's head lolled back, and the tea dribbled down her chin. "Let me help." He sat on the edge of the bed and leaned Ellen against his chest so her head stayed up. Jessica pinched her cheeks to get her mouth to open and managed to dribble a bit of tea down her throat.

"Maybe if you got a cloth and let her suck the tea up."

Jessica brightened. "Good idea." She went to the kitchen and tore a strip of cotton from a clean dishcloth, dipped it in water, and brought it back to the bed. She twisted it and dunked it into the tea, then put it between Ellen's lips.

Ellen sucked on it feebly. "Good," she gasped.

Through the long night they held the basin while she vomited, and they cleaned her and the sheets as often as the diarrhea came. They got as much tea and water down her as they could. The doctor checked on her twice and seemed satisfied with her care.

By dawn they were both exhausted. The skin beneath Jessica's eyes looked bruised from lack of sleep and worry, and Clay figured he looked just as bad. But Ellen looked a little better. He hoped it wasn't wishful thinking.

"Why don't you go home and lie down for a few hours," he suggested to Jessica. "When you come back, I'll catch a few winks."

She hesitated, then nodded. "I want to check on Franny anyway." She stood and stretched. "I'll be back in a couple of hours."

When she opened the door to leave, he called out, "Hey, Red."

She didn't even glare at him when he said the hated nickname. She just gazed back with a question in her eyes.

"You're all right. I guess I was wrong about you. Thanks."

Her face lit with a weary smile. "That's the first time I ever heard a man admit he was wrong."

Clay grinned. "Treasure it then. It may be a long time before you hear it again." Jessica left, then he turned back to Ellen. She was sleeping peacefully with a bit of color in her cheeks, and hope surged.

A few minutes later Doctor Mason opened the door and

walked into the room with dragging feet. Clay could tell he was totally exhausted.

"I think she looks better," Clay said.

The doctor bent over her and put his stethoscope to her chest. "Lungs are clear." He grunted, then straightened and put his stethoscope away. "Today will be crucial if she's going to make it."

Clay's heart sank. He'd hoped they were through the worst of it. "When can we know?"

"When she starts sitting up, taking a bit of food, and is able to keep it down, then she'll be through the worst of it." Doctor Mason picked up his black bag and headed for the door. "I'm going home to try to get a couple hours of sleep. Send someone for me if she gets worse."

After the doctor left, Clay sank to his knees and bowed his head. He pleaded for Ellen's life again and listed all the reasons why God shouldn't take her now. But he couldn't help feeling an overwhelming sense of foreboding.

He stayed on his knees beside her bed and watched her sleep. She breathed easily and deeply. Surely she was going to be all right. He was worrying needlessly. When the door opened behind him, he turned to see Jessica enter. He glanced at his pocket watch. She'd come back in exactly two hours, just as she'd promised.

"Franny is fine. Caleb and Bridie are taking her to play at the Burts'."

"Good." He got to his feet and stretched.

"Has the doctor been back?"

Clay nodded. "He said she wasn't through the woods yet. Today should tell."

Jessica sighed and went to fix some coffee. "It's going to be a long day. You'd better get some rest while she's sleeping."

"I will soon." He grinned as he watched her carefully fix the coffee just the way he'd shown her. Maybe he'd misjudged the selfish beauty. Maybe she really did love Ellen.

Ellen groaned, and Jessica hurried to her side. She held the basin while Ellen was sick again, then wiped her friend's mouth and coaxed a bit more tepid tea down her.

Ellen opened her eyes and looked from Clay to Jessica. "You two been here all night?"

"Where else would we be?" Jessica smoothed Ellen's tangled hair back from her face. "How do you feel?"

"Pretty awful." Her face was nearly as white as the pillow, and a yellow pallor lurked behind the white. "What's wrong with me?"

Clay looked at Jessica, then back at Ellen. He didn't want to tell her, but he couldn't lie to her. "Cholera," he said reluctantly.

Ellen winced as cramps gripped her stomach. "How's Franny?"

"She's fine," Jessica told her. "She was on her way fishing with Caleb and Bridie when I left her a few minutes ago."

Ellen nodded and closed her eyes with a grimace of pain.

"Go get some sleep." Jessica pushed Clay toward the door.

The touch of her hand against his chest made his mouth go dry. He surely wasn't beginning to get attached to her, was he? The light through the window set her hair aflame, and he longed to reach out and touch a shining curl. He could smell the fresh scent of the soap she'd used and the honeysuckle scent she wore. She smelled like sunshine.

She stared up at him with those amazingly blue eyes, and the pulse in her throat began to hammer. *She feels it too. Amazing.* She parted her lips and he bent his head.

As his lips touched hers, it was as if a jolt of lightning ran clear through him. He gripped her shoulders and pulled her closer. The soft feel of her in his arms made him dizzy. He tore his mouth from hers and looked into her bemused face. Her eyes were still half closed.

"I have to go." He pushed her away and ran out the door as though a thousand demons chased him. He had to get away and get his thoughts together. He couldn't love her. She wasn't a Christian. Surely it was just the stress of their shared situation that made him feel such crazy things. They both just needed a little comfort.

Six

Jessica stared at the closed door in disbelief, then touched her fingers to her lips. Clay had actually kissed her! She still felt the shock of his lips on hers. She had flirted with many men, had held their hands and gazed into their eyes, and she had even done the kissing necessary to make another woman jealous. But she'd never *been* kissed where it was a mutual touching of lips and souls. She smiled and spun around the room.

I love him. The thought was overwhelming. So this was what love felt like. That's what the difference in the kiss meant. And surely he must love her, or his kiss would not have felt so amazing. She felt giddy from the revelation of her feelings.

What should she say when he came back? Would he ask her to marry him? She frowned at the thought. She wouldn't like him to be gone a lot. And that's what a traveling preacher did–travel. Perhaps she could contact some of Papa's friends back east and find him a position in a large church somewhere. He was too imposing of a man to be stuck in this backwater.

Her head was filled with visions of a socially prominent life as Clay's wife, and she smiled. She could learn to adjust to hearing about God all the time too. No one would ever know she wasn't a true believer herself.

She rinsed the coffee cups, then went to sit beside Ellen's bed. After a few minutes of daydreaming, her head began to nod. She slid to the floor and leaned her head against the bed. If Ellen needed anything, she would hear her. She drifted to sleep with sweet visions of being in Clay's arms again.

She awoke when the front door banged. Clay came toward her with a frown. "If you were too tired to watch her, you should have said so." He helped Jessica to her feet, and they both turned to check Ellen.

Her mouth and eyes were both open, and a dribble of vomit trailed down her chin. Jessica stared in horror, then reached out and touched her. She was cold. A scream rose in her throat, and she backed away from the bed.

She'd killed her. She had killed her only friend. She put a hand to her mouth, strangling the cry that burst from her lips, then sank limply to the floor and buried her face in her hands.

Clay made a queer, choked sound and gently closed Ellen's eyes. Tears leaked from his eyes, and he struggled to control his emotions.

"I killed her," Jessica sobbed. "If I'd been awake, she wouldn't have died."

"You don't know that," Clay said woodenly. He sat in the chair and leaned his head into his hands. "The doc said it would be touch and go. God decided it was her time. I don't know why. Why would he take Franny's mother and father both within a few months of each other? How do we tell Franny?" It was a cry from the heart.

Jessica sobbed again. How could she bear this pain? Poor Franny. She loved her mother so much.

They stayed motionless, stunned with grief, for several long minutes, then Clay got to his feet and started toward the door. "I'd better notify the doctor. Can you stay with her?"

She nodded. "I'm sorry, Clay. So sorry. It's my fault. All my fault." Grief and guilt gnawed at her insides. She'd never felt such remorse. If she could take her friend's place, she gladly would. How could Clay bear to look at her now? How could she bear to see the accusation in his eyes? "Why wasn't it me? I have nothing. Nobody would care if I died. Why Ellen?"

He turned and looked at her. "Don't blame yourself, Red. We can't know God's ways sometimes. We just have to trust him even when it hurts." He closed the door behind him.

Jessica crawled to the bed where Ellen lay. Her skin was beginning to take on the waxy pallor of death. Just a few days ago they'd sat in this room and laughed. She had told Ellen things she hadn't told anyone before. Why had she never realized before what a blessing it was to have a friend? She didn't think she would ever have another one. It hurt too much to lose one.

Clay came back soon with the doctor, and they wrapped Ellen's body in a sheet and carried it out. The doctor touched her shoulder briefly. "There will be five other funerals tomorrow, Miss DuBois. You did all you could."

Did he think it would comfort her to know others had died

too? She didn't care about the others. She only cared about Ellen. And she *hadn't* done all she could. That's what hurt so much. If she had been awake to help Ellen when she vomited, she would still be alive.

Numbly Jessica gathered up the soiled clothing and bedding and took them out to the pile of laundry in the yard. She looked around at the stacks of clothing and the pot for boiling the clothes. Someone else would take this little cabin and the job Ellen had been so thrilled to get. A sob burst again from Jessica's throat, and she hurried across the parade ground toward home. She wanted to fling herself across her bed and weep until she had no more tears.

Her mother looked up when she burst into the house. Mama put her hand to her mouth. "Oh, my dear girl," she said in a faltering voice. "I feared she wouldn't make it."

Jessica burst into fresh tears, and her mother held her as she sobbed out her grief and misery. Poor Franny. The little girl already knew more about loss than any child should. Jessica lifted her wet face from her mother's shoulder. "Can we take care of Franny, Mama?"

She hesitated a moment, then nodded. "Of course, darling. I'm sure Samuel won't mind if she stays with us for a bit."

"Not just a bit. Always. I want to keep her." Until she spoke the words, she didn't realize she felt that way. She didn't see how she could love Franny any more if she were her own daughter. "Please, Mama."

Her mother gestured around the tiny space. "We have no room, Jessica. You know we're already cramped."

"We can put up a small bed in my room, or she can even sleep with me." But even as she argued, she knew it was no use. Her mother was right. There was barely room for all of them as it was. Franny was just a little girl right now, but she wouldn't stay little forever. But there had to be a way to keep her. Somehow, she would find a way.

"I'll ask your uncle," her mother promised.

But Jessica knew what he would say. He was a stingy man and would see no need to take in Franny when she had a blood relative right here in Fort Bridger. But how could Clay care for a little girl? He was gone for weeks at a time. It would be too hard on Franny if he took her from fort to fort. Maybe an arrangement where they shared her care would work. She bit her lip. But where would Clay keep her? He lived in a cabin even smaller than Ellen's when he was here, and there was no place for Franny there.

Jessica went to her room wearily. She was too tired to think of a solution now, but surely some idea would come to her. She lay down across the top of the bed without bothering to get undressed, thinking she would just close her eyes for a few minutes. Her head throbbed from stress and tears, but every time she closed her eyes, she saw Ellen's face.

She had been lying there for what seemed like only a few minutes when she heard Franny's voice. Jessica got quickly to her feet, smoothed her hair, and went to the parlor.

Clay was there too, with Franny on his lap. He was listening as Franny recounted the day's events to him.

"I tried to find a tadpole for Jessie, but I couldn't find none."

When Jessica came into the room, Franny gave a squeal of delight and slid from Clay's lap. She ran across the floor and flung herself against Jessica's skirts.

Jessica knelt and gathered her close. "Hey, moppet, did you get muddy like I . . . I mean, Ruth did?"

Franny shook her blonde curls. "I stayed clean." She patted Jessica's hair, then touched her face. "Why are you crying? I really tried to find you a tadpole."

The tears rained down Jessica's cheeks harder. "I know you did, sweetie." She muffled a sob. She took a deep breath and looked at Clay helplessly.

He stepped forward, took Franny from Jessica, and brought her to the sofa. Jessica sank beside him and clasped her hands in her lap. "We need to talk to you, sweetie."

The little girl touched his face and looked over at Jessica. Her eyes welled with tears. "Is it Mommy? Did she go to see Jesus too?" Fear settled in her eyes.

Jessica's gaze flew to Clay's face. He looked as astonished as she felt. How had Franny known? She caressed her blonde curls. "Yes, darling. Yes, she did."

Franny buried her face in Clay's chest. "I want my mommy," she wailed. "I don't want Mommy to go see Daddy and Jesus without me." She ground her tiny fists in her eyes and sobbed. "Mommy! Mommy!"

Jessica wanted to sob with her, but she bit her lip and forced back the tears.

Clay hugged her close, and Jessica could hear the tears in his voice. "We didn't want her to go either. But Jesus wanted to see your mommy real bad, and Daddy was missing her so much. Just think how happy they are together again." He hoisted her up so he could look in her eyes. "And you know, we're going to see them again someday."

"When?" she cried. "I want to see them now!"

"We can't go now. But someday we will. Whenever God says it's time."

She cried softly for a while, then rubbed her eyes. "Where will I sleep? Where will I live?"

"With me," Jessica and Clay answered simultaneously. They each stopped and eyed the other.

"We'll talk about this later," Clay said under his breath to Jessica. He ran his palm over Franny's head consolingly. "You can stay here with Jessica for now."

"I want my mommy . . ." Her cries became wails of anguish.

Tears streaming down his own face, Clay rocked her back and forth in his arms until she finally cried herself to sleep. He carried her to the bedroom and laid her in the middle of Jessica's bed.

While he was gone from the room, Jessica marshaled all the reasons she had for keeping Franny with her. She had to make him see reason. Franny needed a woman. She *had* to make him see that somehow.

"Let's sit on the porch," she suggested when he returned.

He inclined his head in agreement and let her lead the way. Neither of them said anything until they were seated on the porch rocking chairs.

"Franny is my cousin," Clay began. "You're no blood relation at all. She needs someone who will love her no matter what. I don't mean to be unkind, but you really have had very little experience with children. You've mostly seen her at her best. The next few months are going to be rough for her while she deals with the loss of both her parents. And I love her. She belongs with me."

"I know everything you say is true. But I love Franny too. I don't see how anyone could love her more than I do." Clay's face softened, and she took hope as she plunged on. "You have to understand, Clay. I was always afraid to open myself up to care about anyone else. I'd been hurt at a young age, and I didn't trust other people. Ellen and Franny changed all that. Ellen was the first and only friend I've ever had. I will never hurt Franny. Never. I would give my life for her." Tears pooled in her eyes after her impassioned speech, but she didn't care. She didn't care about anything but keeping Franny with her. A small part of her wondered why he didn't see the obvious solution. If they married, they could both keep Franny. Did that kiss mean nothing to him?

Clay was silent a moment. "She belongs with me."

"You travel so much–who's going to care for her when you're not here? And you don't have room for her in that tiny cabin anyway."

His restless movements stilled. She could see he hadn't really thought the whole thing through. "Just think about it," she pleaded. "A decision doesn't have to be made yet. Let's get through the funeral, and we'll talk about it some more."

He stood and paced the length of the porch. "All right. But I'm not promising anything."

"Fair enough. Do we know when the funeral is?"

"Tomorrow morning at ten. Ellen's will be first, and then I have five more to do in the afternoon. Do you want to pick out a dress for her to buried in?"

Tears blurred her vision again, and she nodded.

"Fine. I'll be in the infirmary. Bring it there as soon as you can." He turned and walked down the steps.

She watched his long strides across the parade ground. She hoped he might turn and wave, but he just walked to the infirmary and disappeared inside. What had the kiss earlier meant to him? Nothing at all? Or had she killed any affection he might feel for her with her negligence? She was fiercely glad she had never before felt like this about a man. It hurt. It hurt more than anything she had ever experienced. She swallowed hard and got to her feet. She'd better find a dress for Ellen before Franny awoke.

Ellen's cabin still smelled of sickness and death when she opened the door. She walked to the window and threw it open to let in the fresh air. Rummaging through Ellen's few dresses, she couldn't find anything she thought was appropriate. Maybe one of her own could be altered to fit. Ellen was shorter and plumper, but surely something would work.

She went back home and sorted through her own things. At the bottom of her chest, she found a blue silk dress she had been saving for a dance or some other special occasion. The seams were wide and could easily be let out. The length wouldn't matter. She carried it out to the parlor and showed it to her mother, who agreed to see what she could do with it.

Miriam looked on with a supercilious smile. "Useless is what you are. Can't you do anything for yourself?"

Jessica ignored her, but the words hurt. "Can I help do anything?" she asked her mother.

"I do need to put supper on, dear. Could you let the seams out if I show you how?"

Jessica frowned. She felt all thumbs with a needle. "I can try," she said with reluctance. At least it was better than trying to cook supper herself.

Her mother gave her a pair of tiny scissors and showed her how to snip the threads without harming the delicate fabric, but Jessica still spent an hour just letting out all the seams in the bodice, waist, and arms. At last she laid the dress across the sofa and went to the kitchen. "Thanks, Mama. Is there anything I can do to help you?"

"Ooh, mademoiselle is willing to soil her lily-white hands in the kitchen," Miriam sneered.

Jessica was too tired to think of a good rejoinder, so she just shrugged and took the plates her mother held out to her. She set the table, all the while aware of Miriam's resentful glare. Jessica had thought they were getting along better. Why was her cousin acting like this now? She didn't need this aggravation today.

"I know what you're planning, and it won't work," Miriam said finally.

"I don't have any idea what you're talking about." Jessica picked up the silverware and set it beside the plates.

"You think you'll catch Clay by taking in Franny. But he won't be trapped that easily." Miriam tossed her head. "He told Caleb you weren't his type."

Fresh tears clogged Jessica's throat, and she swallowed hard. She wasn't about to let Miriam see how her words hurt. Rather than risk having her voice quiver, she said nothing at all and continued with her chore. Irritated that her taunt had gone unanswered, Miriam muttered under her breath and stormed from the room.

"That's really not why you want Franny, is it, dear?"

Carefully Jessica laid the last setting on the table and turned to face her mother. "Would you really believe that I would do something like that, Mama?"

She had her answer in the flash of uncertainty that crossed her mother's face. "I'm going for a walk." Jessica whirled and practically ran from the room. Was that how everyone saw her? As a conniver and deceiver? She hurried across the parade ground to Ellen's cabin, where she sat at the familiar battered kitchen table. In the peace and quiet there she faced her own nature.

She *had* done things like that before. No wonder that's what people thought now. She remembered her unholy alliance with Ben Croftner and how they had arranged for Sarah Campbell to be handed over to the Sioux. How she had investigated Emmie's background and threatened to tell Isaac all about how she hadn't really been married to her first husband.

Jessica had done a lot of bad, even evil, things in her life. She wasn't proud of them, and she didn't really know why she had done them. At the time it had just seemed important to win. Saving face and getting what she wanted had once been the most important things to her.

She wasn't even sure how or when the change in her had begun. Papa's death had probably been the beginning. Seeing the goodness in Emmie and Sarah back at Fort Phil Kearny had made her yearn to be better herself, even though she had hated to admit it. But the main relationship that had changed her was her friendship with Ellen and Franny. Ellen had been so good, so caring. Jessica wished she could be like her, but no amount of good intentions would bring about such a miraculous transformation. She would, however, try to be a better person. She would care for Franny and perhaps somehow atone for Ellen's death.

She gave a heavy sigh. Clay's kiss was another thing that had changed her. But apparently it had meant nothing to him. He showed no sign that the moment had even touched him. She squeezed her eyes shut, then got to her feet and slowly went back home. Life was so complicated, so hard. Where was her relationship with Clay going?

The next morning the leaden sky looked as heavy as Jessica's heart felt. She curled Franny's hair and dressed her in her best dress. The little girl's face was peaked and woeful, and Jessica's heart broke for this small child who had to face such sorrow. She clung to Jessica's hand, and they made their way to the officers' rec room where the funeral would be held.

The small room was packed with enlisted men. None of the officers' wives had come, except Jessica's mother, and Jessica felt a sharp stab of anger that they would continue with their snobbery in the face of this tragedy. Her cousins' and uncle's presence gave her a warm glow of gratitude, though. Maybe this was what family was all about, sticking by one another in times of tragedy and heartache.

The funeral was brief. Jessica tried not to watch Clay, but his grief was evident. He almost broke down several times during the service. Franny cried the entire time. After the service Jessica took Franny back to the house and tucked her into bed for a nap. Clay had said he would be over after the other funerals. There would be just one mass funeral for the men who had died of cholera, so he shouldn't be more than an hour or so.

She found it hard to wait. She wanted to keep Franny so badly, but what if Clay said no? Restless, she followed her mother into the kitchen. "Did you talk to Uncle Samuel about Franny?" She had a feeling she already knew what he had said. Her mother had been uncharacteristically quiet since they got back from the funeral.

Her mother bit her lip. "I'm sorry, darling, but there just isn't room to keep Franny permanently. Of course, she can stay until Reverend Cole can make arrangements for her."

Jessica blinked furiously to keep the tears at bay. She had to make them see how important this was to her. But before she could marshal her arguments, someone knocked on the front door. Her heart pounding, she raced to the door and flung it open.

"Jessica." Clay took off his hat. His eyes were grave and

shadowed with grief. He followed her into the parlor. "Where's Franny?"

"Napping. She was exhausted from crying." She showed him to a seat and went to fetch them both a cup of coffee.

"I'll let you discuss Franny's situation with Reverend Cole alone," her mother whispered. "I need to make a call on Mrs. McNeil. She's feeling a bit poorly. I'll be back in about an hour." She took her bonnet and left to make her call.

Jessica took the coffee and ambled back to the parlor. She felt a sense of futility and trepidation. Clay wasn't going to let her keep Franny. She tried to tell herself she was jumping to conclusions, but somehow she just knew. She handed Clay a cup of coffee, then sat in the chair facing him.

He took a gulp of coffee and stared down into it morosely. "I wish Ellen had some family I could notify about her death, but her parents are both dead and I have no idea where her brother is." He took another gulp of coffee and finally raised his gaze to her face. "I've prayed about your request to keep Franny," he said after a long moment of staring into her eyes. He set his cup on the table beside him and stood. "I have a lot of reservations about it." He paced from the fireplace to the sofa and back again.

"Why? Surely you can see that a little girl needs a woman around." Perhaps he hadn't decided against her plans after all. Her heart began to pound with hope.

Clay nodded. "I know you love her, Red, but love isn't everything." He took a deep breath. "She also needs a Christian upbringing, to be taught solid spiritual values, to be introduced to

Jesus when she's ready. Franny needs to know that if she wants to see her mother again, only Jesus can do that for her. Can you teach her those things?"

Jessica tried to speak, but what could she say?

"I know you don't have much use for God, and that's a very important issue. I don't want Franny to grow up thinking God doesn't matter." He stared at his hands a moment and raked his fingers through his hair. "Another thing is the matter of her support. If you keep her, your stepfather would be the one providing her support. I could help, but he would have the ultimate responsibility. She'd be a charity case, and I really don't want that for her. So I've come up with a plan that might solve all of our problems, but I don't think you'll agree. I'm not sure you could even do it." His tone was ominous.

Jessica jumped to her feet. "I can do anything if it means I can keep Franny with me!"

Clay gave a wry grin. "I don't think so, Red. The only way I can agree to let Franny stay with you is if *you* provide her support yourself by taking over Ellen's job as post laundress. We would have family devotions when I'm here, and when I'm not here, you'll teach her about God yourself with some lessons I'll leave for you."

Jessica gaped at him. "Me? Post laundress?" Her voice rose and ended in a squeak. It was ludicrous. How could he even ask her to do such a thing? "You must be mad." The strength left her legs, and she sank back into the chair.

"I didn't think you'd agree, but those are my terms. It's the only way I'll agree to let you raise Franny."

Jessica knew he wouldn't budge from his position. But it was ridiculous. Even if she agreed, which she wouldn't, she didn't even know *how* to do laundry.

"If she stayed here, she would just be another burden on your mother. If you want her, *you* have to be the one who does the work. This is a job you can't pass off on someone else."

Jessica leaped to her feet and jabbed her finger at him. "Now I understand. This is just your way of pointing out how worthless you think I am. You had no intention of letting me keep Franny, did you? You just wanted to humiliate me." Tears choked her, and she was so angry, she couldn't think of anything else to say.

"I'm sorry you see it that way. But those are my terms."

She put her hands on her hips. "Well, I won't do it. And I still intend to keep Franny." *Just let him try to take her.*

Clay shrugged. "I'm sorry, Red. I'll take Franny now."

"You will not. She's sleeping."

But she wasn't. Her blonde head peeked around the corner, and then she ran to Clay. Her face was screwed with grief as he gathered her against his chest. "Hey, muffin. You ready to go home with me?"

She gave a sob and nodded. "I want Molly." Her voice was muffled against his chest.

"When I left her she was lying on the bed waiting for you to come play with her." He turned around and started for the door.

There was nothing Jessica could do, short of dragging Franny from him bodily. She watched helplessly as he gave her one last penetrating glance before he carried Franny out the door. She stared after him in disbelief, then burst into tears.

She hated to cry. It made her feel weak and out of control, but she couldn't seem to help herself lately. She suddenly hated Clay with a fierce passion. How dare he sit in judgment on her? This was all because she was beautiful, and he didn't trust beautiful women. She would be a good mother to Franny. Why couldn't he see that?

She refused supper and stayed in her room when the family came home. She was still awake when her cousins came to bed later. She pretended to be sleeping because she didn't want to hear Miriam's smug comments about Clay refusing to let her raise Franny.

When morning came, she hadn't slept at all. The six o'clock call for reveille rang out, and she slipped out of bed. She would do it. There was simply no other way. Clay wasn't about to change his mind, but she would show him what kind of backbone she had. She quietly dressed and slipped out of the house to find him. She thought he would be at Ellen's cabin, and the light shining through the window proved she was right.

Clay opened the door almost instantly at her knock. He stared at her for a moment and then gave her a slow smile. "Couldn't sleep, Red?"

She brushed by him without answering, then turned to face him. "I'll do it."

His jaw dropped, but he quickly recovered. "It won't be easy."

"I don't have any choice."

"Sure you do." He frowned and thrust his hands in his pockets. "You can be sensible and go back to your mother's house and forget all about this nonsense."

"That's what you'd hoped I'd do, wasn't it? You thought I'd never agree to your little test, and you could just do as you pleased with Franny." She poked a finger in his chest. "But I can take anything you throw my way, Clay Cole. I'll prove to you I can do whatever it takes to provide a home for Franny." She shoved past him and poured herself a cup of coffee. "Now get out of my house and leave me in peace."

Clay stared at her, consternation written across his face. He closed his mouth, picked up his hat, and turned to the door. "Franny didn't get much sleep last night, so you might let her sleep in this morning. I'll notify Colonel Edwards that you will be accepting the position. There's plenty of laundry waiting to be done, so you'd better get to work." He clapped his hat on his head and shut the door behind him.

Jessica stared at the closed door, then around her at the tiny cabin and the duffel bags full of dirty laundry heaped in the corner. What had she done?

Seven

The strong smell of lye and soap hung like a moist veil in the heavy air. Jessica blinked against the sting of the fumes and tried to encourage the fire by poking at it with a stick. It responded momentarily with a flare of flame, then settled down to a dull glow again. How did one go about getting the stupid thing to burn anyway? She blew a strand of hair out of her eyes and sighed as she turned toward the door to check on Franny.

The little girl still slept, and Jessica breathed another sigh, this one of relief. Since Clay had left an hour ago, she'd piled the logs in the stove and fetched bucket after bucket of water. But the fire refused to burn hot enough to dissolve the soap properly, and her determination was fast deserting her. She felt like bursting into tears at the enormity of the task. She had never washed a single article of clothing in her life and really didn't know the first thing about how to start. She wasn't even sure she had put the right amount of soap in the water. She had just dumped until she thought it smelled strong enough to clean. She wished she could consult her mother, but Franny was still asleep, and she couldn't leave her alone.

How had she let Clay manipulate her into this fix? She poked at the fire again. It responded this time by sending out small flames that began to lick eagerly at the piled wood. She gave a smile of triumph and dumped the first gunnysack of clothing onto the ground. She'd seen Ellen soak the clothing in the big tub, but other times she'd seen her scrubbing things on an old washboard in the smaller tub. Which came first?

While she stood contemplating her chore, Miriam came by with Anne Dials, the young wife of Lieutenant Billy Dials. Both young women stopped and looked at Jessica in amazement.

"What on earth are you doing?" Miriam demanded, leaning against the fence.

"What does it look like?" Jessica pushed the hair out of her eyes again. "I'm the newest laundress for Fort Bridger. I told you yesterday I was going to do this."

Miriam's mouth opened like a fish, but no sound came out. "I didn't believe you were serious!" she gasped finally.

Jessica scowled at her. "Does it look like I'm joking?"

Anne giggled behind her hand, and Miriam reddened. "Wait until your mother and my father hear about this." She tossed her head. "You can't do this. It's embarrassing!" She stalked away. Anne followed with a last pitying glance toward Jessica.

"Tell Mama I need to see her." Jessica shouted after them. The contempt in Anne's eyes had stung. Jessica had been too defiant and angry with Clay earlier to remember how lowly a laundress was in the eyes of the women here. Heat rose in her face. She didn't care what someone like Anne Dials thought about her.

The water was bath-warm when her mother came hurrying across the parade ground. "Miriam told me what was going on over here," she gasped. "You can't do this, Jessica. It's much too hard for you. You've never even washed a single article of clothing."

"I'll learn." Jessica stirred the soap and explained the deal she had struck with Clay. Her mother was silent throughout her narrative, but Jessica thought a hint of a smile might have come and gone on her mother's face. What was there to smile about? There was nothing remotely funny about this situation. She scowled at her mother and turned abruptly toward the pile of laundry.

"Can you explain how I'm supposed to do this wash?" She kicked at a pair of dungarees at her feet. They were heavily stained with grass and mud. How was she supposed to get those stains out?

Mama fluttered her hands. "Oh dear. Let me see what to tell you first. Put the clothes in the pot to soak some of the soil loose. Then you agitate them with this." She pointed to a paddle against the wall. "Other stains have to be scrubbed on the washboard." She stayed for about an hour and showed Jessica what to do.

A sentry shouted the time, and Mama put her hand to her mouth. "I must go. Samuel will be home for his lunch soon. I'll check back this afternoon to see if you're having any problems."

She scurried away, pausing once to look back with a strange look on her face, a mixture of pride and exasperation. But Jessica certainly didn't feel any pride in what she'd agreed to do, although she felt plenty of exasperation.

She had just hung the first batch of clothes on the line when

Franny came out the door, rubbing her eyes sleepily. She stumbled across the muddy yard and hooked her hand in Jessica's skirt. "Where's Uncle Clay?"

"He had to go to work, sweetheart. He'll be back after supper. I'm going to stay here and take care of you."

The little girl's blue eyes grew enormous. "Forever and ever? Just like Mommy did?" Two giant tears rolled down her cheeks.

Answering tears stung Jessica's eyes. "Forever and ever." She knelt and took Franny in her arms. "Your mommy was a wonderful mommy, and I know I can't be as good a mommy as she was, but I'm going to try to take care of you like she would have wanted." The feel of those chubby arms around her neck made the last hour's work worthwhile.

She put Franny back on the ground and took her hand. "How about some lunch?" They walked back to the cabin, and Jessica sat the little girl on a chair at the table. "What sounds good to eat?"

Jessica looked at the meager supplies. She would have to see about getting some food. There were some dried beans she could cook for supper, a bit of salt pork, two slices of bread, and a few shriveled potatoes. "How about some jam and bread?" There didn't seem to be much else to fix.

"I love jam." Franny leaned her chin against her hand and watched as Jessica spread butter and jam on the last remaining bread slices.

As they ate their lunch, Jessica watched the dimples in Franny's cheeks come and go and felt content. After she finished with the laundry, she would try her hand at baking some bread.

Mama had promised to come back, and maybe she could take time to show her how.

After their meager lunch she put the beans in a pan and covered them with water the way she had seen her mother do. She put the pot on the cookstove and got the fire going, relieved that it was a bit more cooperative than the one in the yard. Feeling pleased with herself, she took Franny and her doll out to the yard and settled her in a corner of the laundry tent while Jessica tackled another load of dirty clothing.

A mere hour later she wasn't feeling so complacent. Her back and arms ached from bending over the tub, and her head hurt from the fumes. Red, chapped areas on her hands itched almost unbearably, and Franny was beginning to whine from boredom. Her mother had stopped by, but only briefly, and Jessica felt abandoned and alone. How was she supposed to get all this work done? The thought of doing this every day made her shudder. She was thankful the tent offered meager protection from the sun, although she still had to stand in the sun to stir the clothes in the tub over the fire.

She straightened wearily and put a hand to her back. After fetching Franny some blocks, she hung clothes on the line and gathered up another armload of laundry.

"Hey, Red, you look tired." Clay's wide grin was insufferably smug. "Ready to give up this crazy idea?"

Although that was exactly what she'd been thinking, Jessica straightened her shoulders and lifted her chin. "Of course not. I'm getting along just fine. You really don't need to check up on me."

His grin widened. "You look done in. Want some help?"

Torn between her pride and her common sense, Jessica hesitated. She was relieved when Franny ran up to Clay and distracted him.

He picked her up and tossed her into the air. "How would you and Molly like to go to the sutler's store for a piece of licorice?" He cocked an eyebrow at Jessica. "That okay with you?"

"Of course. I was about to suggest you spend some time with her. Watching me do laundry isn't much fun for her." So much for his offer of help. Not that she would have let him know she could use the assistance, of course.

"Now you know why Ellen was so grateful for those days you took Franny with you." He settled his hat more firmly on his head and turned to go, then turned back toward her. "I'll be over about seven for devotions with you and Franny. That should give you time to get supper done and Franny bathed and settled."

"Why don't you come for supper?" As soon as the words were out, she wished them back. What had possessed her to invite him? She was exhausted, her back hurt, and this was her first attempt at cooking a meal. She bit her lip and looked away. Maybe he would refuse.

But he grinned again, that devastating smile that did funny things to her stomach, and nodded. "It's a deal." He gave her a small wave and left her alone with her thoughts.

She squeezed her eyes shut, and two lone tears trickled from behind her closed eyelids. She would get through this. There were men here, lots of men. She needed to think about finding one who would get her out of this situation. It shouldn't be too hard.

Her thoughts strayed to that single kiss she'd shared with Clay. If only he loved her as she loved him . . . But that was just a trap. Love meant nothing. She needed to find a man before this work destroyed her beauty.

Clay shook his head as he strode across the parade ground. He had been shocked when Jessica agreed to his demands and even more amazed when she started actually doing the dirty laundry. He hadn't realized how incongruous the picture of her bending over a tub of laundry was until he saw her do it. The sleeves of her expensive gown had been pushed up to reveal the smooth, white skin of her arms, and her hair, usually so carefully coiffed, hung in strings around her flushed face. Her flawless complexion was now dusted with freckles from the sun.

Red had a lot more gumption than he'd given her credit for. He had actually felt sorry for her when he saw her bending over that tub, but he had hardened his heart. She needed to learn this lesson. He didn't want Franny raised by a high-society debutante.

A memory of the way she had felt in his arms stirred him, and he pushed it away. It was a never-to-be-repeated moment of madness, a temporary wave of insanity. They had too many differences, and the main one was her lack of faith in God. If she ever thought she could twist him around her finger, she'd have him tucking his tail between his legs and meekly agreeing to pastor some high-society church back east somewhere.

She didn't understand his calling and never would. His father had worked himself to death to try to satisfy Clay's beautiful mother, but nothing had been enough for her. Clay had vowed never to be the milquetoast his father had been.

He and Franny bought a stick of licorice, then strolled around the fort. Several soldiers hailed him, and he stopped for a chat each time. He helped one soldier upright an overturned wagon, then took Franny to visit Lieutenant Brown's wife, Charlotte. She had recently given birth to a daughter, and Franny was fascinated with the red-faced, wrinkled baby. He had to admit it was a cute little mite, and he remembered when Franny looked like that. For a moment a vision of Jessica with a baby–his baby–in her arms swept over him, but he quickly dismissed it. *That* would certainly never happen.

Mrs. Brown insisted they stay for tea, and it was nearly six when he took Franny and hurried across the grassy knoll to Suds Row.

The acrid smell of burned beans escaped from under the closed door, and he could hear Jessica banging pots. Good thing he wasn't really hungry after eating with Mrs. Brown.

He knocked on the door and waited several minutes, then knocked again when she didn't answer the door. After another long moment the door swung open, and she motioned him in. She had made an attempt to make herself presentable, but she was still flushed and a bit bedraggled. Dried soap speckled her dress, and freckles stood out on her sunburned face and arms.

"Smells like supper is done," he said with a grin.

She glared at him, then burst into tears. "You're making fun of me, and I've tried so hard today." She scrubbed at her eyes like a child and turned her back to him.

For just a moment he wanted to turn her around and hold her against his chest. What a crazy thought. There was no way he was letting his emotions get involved with her. A beauty like her could take a man's heart and rip it to shreds. She couldn't be as vulnerable as she seemed. He tried to think of something funny to say to defuse the tears, but his mind went blank.

Franny tugged on Jessica's skirt. "Don't cry, Jessie. I brought you a piece of licorice." She held up the candy with a bright smile on her face. "See?"

Jessica looked down at the little girl, then sniffed back the tears. She took the licorice and attempted a watery smile. "How did you know licorice is my favorite candy?"

Clay grinned at the quick recovery of her composure, but his eyes watered from the smoke in the cabin, and he wanted to get away from it. "Let's go for a walk while the cabin clears out." He opened the window.

Her blue eyes filled with tears again, but she just nodded. "I need to go by my mother's and get my things." She followed him out the door, and they turned toward the row of officers' quarters.

Clay felt tongue-tied in her presence. The sharp-tongued, confident Jessica he could handle, but he wasn't so sure about this weepy, uncertain one. This was what he wanted, wasn't it? To humble her a bit and make her take a good hard look at herself? But this new Jessica was more intriguing than the other one, and he wasn't sure he dared to know her better.

They stopped at the DuBois quarters, and Clay and Franny sat on the porch while Jessica went inside to get her things. Miriam and Bridie joined them a few minutes later.

Miriam gave him a flirtatious smile and swished her skirts as she sat beside him. "I haven't seen you for ages," she said with a reproachful look.

"I've been pretty busy. And you won't see me at all for the next few weeks. I leave tomorrow for Utah."

She pouted prettily. "Will you miss me at all?"

He grinned. "I'll be too busy to miss anyone."

Bridie interrupted. "Is Jessica really going to be a washerwoman? Miriam said she saw her doing laundry, but I didn't believe her."

"I don't think she'd like that title very well, but yeah, she is going to be doing laundry."

Bridie's green eyes danced with amusement. "I'll have to stop by and see this for myself."

Jessica came out of the house with an armload of clothing. "I have a trunk of things too. Do you think you could get it to the cabin for me?"

"No problem." He found the small trunk just inside the door and hoisted it to his shoulder. "What you got in here? Books?"

Jessica smiled. "Actually, there are some books in there. I wanted to continue Franny's education."

"Just when do you think you'll have time for that? Even Ellen didn't have time to do everything."

She spun around to face him and put her hands on her hips. "Are you insinuating that I can't do the things Ellen did?"

He started across the parade ground without answering her. If he told her what he really thought, she would just get more riled. She was a high-society do-gooder and would soon tire of this role. In the meantime he would take the help she offered and let Franny enjoy her company.

He had to admit that she'd stuck it out longer than he thought she would. She definitely had pluck. He had thought he'd find her and Franny back at the DuBois quarters by nightfall. He felt a little uneasy at the thought of leaving her for two weeks. He didn't think she would do anything to hurt Franny, but still . . .

She scurried to catch up with him. Pausing when he reached the little bridge across the stream in the middle of the parade ground, he shifted the trunk to the other shoulder and hurried on toward Suds Row. He just wanted to get her settled and leave before he weakened and kissed her again. He thought about that kiss a lot. Too much for his own peace of mind.

The sharp smell of smoke had dissipated some when he shoved open the door and deposited his burden in the corner of the room. Jessica laid her armload of clothing on the bed and eyed him warily. She bit her full lower lip, and he thought again about that kiss. What was wrong with him? Why couldn't he forget it? He stepped away and turned his back on her.

These sudden surges of attraction had to stop. She was not anywhere near his ideal of a suitable wife. He was glad he would be leaving for a few weeks. Maybe by the time he came back, these compelling bouts of tenderness would be gone.

He cleared his throat, then held out his arms to Franny. "Give me a kiss, muffin. I have to go away for a little while."

Franny's eyes filled with tears, and her lips trembled. She flung herself into his chest and wound her arms around his neck. "You can't leave me, Uncle Clay! Please, please, don't go!" Heart-wrenching sobs racked her shoulders, and her tears soaked through his shirt.

"Hey, don't take on so." He smoothed her hair back from her forehead. "I won't be gone long. And Jessica will be here with you. She'll take good care of you."

But his comforting words did little to still the storm of tears. He patted her and looked helplessly at Jessica. She moved to his side and caressed Franny's back.

"How about if Uncle Clay reads you a story before he goes?"

Slowly Franny lifted her face, red and blotched with tear-stains. "The one about the little red hen?"

"I can cluck with the best of them," Clay said with a solemn voice. "You get in your nightie first, and when you're ready for bed, I'll demonstrate my wondrous hen imitation."

She giggled and slid out of his arms to the floor. "Can Molly listen too?"

"If you promise she won't laugh at my clucking."

She laughed again and ran off to change. Clay gave Jessica a grin and a mock sigh. "Now look what you've gotten me into, Red."

"I'm not the one who offered to cluck." Her lips twitched. She looked weary, but her blue eyes were full of mischief. "I wouldn't miss this for anything."

He read two stories to Franny, then took out his Bible. "Time for devotions."

Jessica's eyes widened and she looked away. It was easy to see that spiritual things made her uneasy. He was curious about her background. Her mother faithfully attended the services and seemed truly interested in learning all she could about God. How had that spiritual hunger missed Jessica? Ellen had hinted that he should get to know her better before judging her. Was there some secret from Jessica's childhood that had shaped her?

He shook the musings away and opened his well-thumbed Bible. He decided to start with something easy and turned to Psalm 23. He read the psalm to Franny and helped her learn the first two verses.

Jessica listened closely and seemed determined to participate in this facet of Franny's upbringing. "Is there such a thing as still waters in this life?" she asked him after they put Franny to bed. "My experience has been that turbulence and trouble follow us everywhere we go. Look at what happened to Ellen."

"True. But when we have God, we can rest in him and know that he has everything under control, even when we can't see it."

She was silent a moment. "Did God want Franny to be orphaned?"

"You ask hard questions. God never promised we wouldn't have trouble and problems in this life. He just promised to go with us through them." He stopped and stared down at her.

That wasn't good enough for her, and she shook her head. "You'll have to explain that."

He sighed. "As parents we would like to spare our children any hardship and trials, but if we were able to shield our child from any hard blow, she would grow up spoiled and selfish with no idea how to take care of herself, with no compassion for the pain of others, and with the thought that the world revolved around her. God is much too wise and loves us too much to ever make that mistake. The hard things in life shape us and mold us into a closer picture of Jesus. Our goal here should be to become more like him. We can't do that if God shields us from every bump and bruise."

He could see her thinking about his words. "You're describing me, aren't you?" she said finally. "You think I'm spoiled and selfish and that my parents coddled me too much. You really don't know about the bruises and bumps I had early in life."

Clay was quiet for a moment. "We can choose to let those bruises shape us into someone better, or we can use them as an excuse for willful, selfish behavior."

Jessica stood and turned her back to him. "At least now I know what you really think about me. You'd better go. I'm tired and I need to go to bed."

He picked up his hat and jammed it on his head, then took his Bible and rose to his feet. "Just remember what I said, Red. Only you can decide whether to let those painful memories help you or heal you."

Her eyes were shadowed with fatigue and defiance, but she followed him to the door.

"I'll be back in a few weeks, and I'll try to take Franny off your hands as much as possible during the day. If you need anything, you can send a telegram to Fort Douglas."

She didn't answer him but only inclined her head. He looked at her stiff shoulders and sighed. He hadn't meant to hurt her, but maybe she was beginning to see herself. She had at least recognized that she was spoiled and selfish. Maybe when he got back they could talk more.

Eight

Jessica slammed the shirt she was washing against the side of the tub, then scrubbed it viciously against the washboard. The hapless shirt was taking the brunt of her anger and hurt after her talk with Clay. He'd been gone a month, but his remarks still rankled. She couldn't seem to get them out of her mind. There were plenty of men around here who admired both her beauty and her spirit, so why was she pining away for a man who cared for neither?

Officers and enlisted men came by daily, and the fort was inundated with men stopping through on their way to the goldfields or the West Coast, men who had cast appreciative glances her way. She could snap her fingers and have soft and white hands. They now looked like they belonged to someone else–red and freckled with itchy patches, her nails broken and ragged. Someday when she was back in Boston, this would be like a dream. She and Franny would wear gloves and take tea with people of culture.

Her heart ached at the knowledge that her future would not include Clay. He might make it back east once in a while to see Franny, but he had made it clear that his future didn't include Jessica.

She hung the last of the clothing on the line and went to the cabin with lagging steps. Franny followed her with her doll Molly. She had been unusually quiet today, and Jessica knew she missed her mother. Jessica spent a little extra time cuddling her after supper, then read her a story and put her to bed.

She thought again about her situation. What she should do is find a man to marry her, one who would be willing to be a father to Franny. Once the idea took root, she smiled. That wouldn't be hard to do. But not a soldier! Perhaps one of the emigrants on their way to California or Oregon. She'd heard it was beautiful along the coast. Suddenly Boston didn't seem so attractive. A man would solve all her problems.

The next morning Jessica awoke determined to put her plan into action. She slipped her best dress over her head, arranged her hair in becoming curls, and applied a touch of rouge to her cheeks. Franny watched in fascination as Jessica transformed herself.

"Now it's your turn, sweetie." She put a ruffled blue dress on the little girl and pulled the soft blonde curls back in a ribbon. How long had it been since she'd taken the time to attend to Franny like this? She bit her lip. So much for being the perfect mother.

She took Franny's hand and went to the door. "Let's go to the bakery and buy you a sticky bun."

Franny's eyes grew wide. "Just for me?"

"All for you."

Quite a little town had sprung up in recent months. Fort Bridger had turned into a major stopping-off place for emigrants and prospectors. Jessica almost felt as though she didn't know the place anymore. Clay had said it wouldn't be long until it was a regular town. She was aware of people's stares as they walked past the various shops and businesses.

A tall, handsome, middle-aged gentleman took off his hat and bowed as she passed. "Ma'am."

"It's miss," Jessica said with her most fetching smile.

He was immediately fetched. "Robert Ketcham, at your service, Miss, eh . . . ?"

Jessica held out her gloved hand. "Miss Jessica DuBois," she said with a demure flutter of her lashes. "I'm so pleased to meet you, Mr. Ketcham. This is my ward, Franny."

Robert knelt and took Franny's small hand. "Hello, Franny. Would you like a licorice stick?"

She looked up at Jessica, then shook her head. "We're going to get me a sticky bun. One just for me."

"A sticky bun it will be then." He offered Jessica his elbow. "May I?"

She smiled again in a way to make her dimple appear. "Why, thank you, sir. How kind."

"Please, call me Robert." He escorted her down the street to the bakery and held open the door for her.

Robert was attentive throughout their breakfast. He was a businessman on his way to California, and he told Jessica all about his factories in New York and Pennsylvania. "When my wife died, I decided to expand my concerns to the West. It seemed a good time to see something of the world while profiting at the same time.

Unfortunately we had no children, so there was nothing to keep me back east."

He's perfect. Jessica debated about how much to tell him and finally decided on the truth. He would have to know about her circumstances sooner or later.

"My father, Major DuBois, was killed in the Fetterman disaster last December. Mama was forced to marry his brother when Papa died without enough money for her to support us." She told him all about Ellen and how much she loved Franny and just what she'd agreed to do to keep her.

Robert's eyes were fixed on her face through her entire explanation. She could see the admiration intensify as her tale unfolded. Just as she'd hoped.

"You're a remarkable woman, my dear. You deserve a bit of enjoyment after all you've been through. May I take you and young Franny to dinner tonight?"

She allowed herself just a moment of hesitation so he wouldn't realize his invitation was exactly what she'd been waiting for. "Why, that's very kind of you, Robert. I think we can squeeze that in. It sounds delightful."

His face reddened and he smiled. "Shall I call for you about six?"

She inclined her head. "We'll be ready."

He took her gloved hand and pressed his lips to it. "I look forward to it with great anticipation." His dark eyes gleamed as he escorted her to the door.

She could feel his gaze on her all the way down the street, but she resisted the impulse to turn to make sure. Smiling inside, she forced herself to walk sedately, even though she felt like skipping. She had known it would be easy, but she hadn't expected to find someone so cultured and rich the very first day.

When they reached the cabin, she changed her clothes and popped Franny into a play dress. "Did you like Mr. Ketcham?"

Franny nodded. "But I like Uncle Clay more. When is he coming back to see us?"

When, indeed? Jessica had expected him last week. But when he finally showed his face, she was determined he would not find her pining away for him. When he saw her on Robert's arm, he'd realize what he'd lost.

Since she was anticipating the pleasure of an evening out with an admiring man, the day flew by. Even the daunting task of the laundry didn't dampen her spirits. Franny played happily in the shade of the tent while Jessica scrubbed the clothes. October was almost here, and winter wouldn't be far off. She would need to move quickly with Robert in order to get out of here before the snows fell in the mountains to the west.

She tried not to think about Clay. She was determined to put that madness behind her. Somehow she would forget him and go on with her life.

She finished her day's work around five and hurried inside with Franny to get cleaned up for their evening out. She hauled and heated water for the small hip bath by the fire, then bathed herself and Franny before dumping the water out the back door. She dressed Franny as she had this morning, then surveyed her own wardrobe, debating for a few minutes over what to wear.

She wanted to look demure yet alluring because she had to hook Robert quickly.

She finally settled on a blue satin dress with a daring neckline, pearl buttons running up the sleeves, and a flounced hemline. She curled her hair again and applied rouge to both her cheeks and her lips. After peering in the hand mirror, she was satisfied with her appearance.

She turned at a knock on the door. Luckily she was ready. She smoothed one last stray hair and hurried to the door. Her welcoming smile froze when she swung open the door and stared into Clay's hazel eyes. Her heart clenched with the shock even as Franny shrieked and flung herself against his legs.

"Uncle Clay, Uncle Clay!" She tried to climb his pant leg, and he scooped her up and held her high.

"How's my girl? Did you miss me?" He settled her against his shoulder and stared down at Jessica.

"We missed you most awfully, didn't we, Jessie?" Franny patted his cheeks. "I don't want you to ever go away again."

He patted her absently while his gaze probed Jessica's face. She flushed at his appraisal. Why did he affect her like this? She didn't like the feeling. Men were the ones who were supposed to gasp at the sight of her. She wanted to be the one in control. She swallowed the lump in her throat.

"When did you get in?" She stepped aside so he could enter.

"Just now. I came straight here. I thought I might catch you before you fixed supper and take you both to Bridger Inn for dinner."

"We already have a dinner engagement."

A tiny muscle tightened in his jaw, but he nodded. "That explains the finery. I thought maybe you'd heard I was back." He gazed down at Franny. "It looks like it's just you and me, muffin. May I have the honor of your presence at dinner?"

Franny squeezed him around the neck. "I told Jessie I liked you better than Mr. Ketcham." She planted a kiss on his chin. "I missed you."

"I missed you too." He looked at Jessica. "Who's Mr. Ketcham, Red?"

She tossed her hair. "Robert is a very wealthy gentleman from New York. He's due here any minute. I'd appreciate it if you would leave before he arrives."

"Ashamed of him?"

"Of course not!" she snapped. "I just don't relish the thought of having you look down your nose at my friends."

"I don't care who you see as long as you realize that Franny's welfare comes first. I should have expected you to cave in as soon as my back was turned. You're not the type to stick with anything for long. I can find other arrangements for Franny."

"What do you mean? I have no intention of giving up Franny!" Her heart began to pound. Surely he wouldn't go back on their agreement.

"The deal was that you would stay here and care for Franny with money you'd earned with your own hands, that you would raise her by Christian standards." He turned to the door. "We'll talk about this later. I'm disappointed in you, Red." He wheeled with Franny in his arms and stalked out the door.

Jessica stared at the shut door. Tears pricked her eyes, and she blinked them back fiercely. She wouldn't cry. If he would insist that she work such long, hard hours, he obviously cared nothing about her. Most men coddled and protected women. But not Reverend Clay Cole. Oh no. He thought a woman should work at a humiliating job that left her sweaty and exhausted. Well, she'd had enough of him and his strange ideas for one day.

She lifted her head at the knock on the door and fixed a smile on her face. Some men knew how to treat a woman, so why was she wasting her tears on a man like Clay? He wasn't worth it.

Furious, Clay strode toward the hotel with Franny in his arms. As soon as his back was turned, Jessica had reverted to her old ways. A man was always the solution for a woman like her. Just when he was beginning to hope she might really have some beauty inside that pretty head, she proved him wrong. He knew he seemed cruel and uncaring, but she had some lessons to learn. She would never grow if all she had to do was bat her beautiful blue eyes and some man would fall all over himself to meet her every wish. How would she ever realize her need for God when she never went without her slightest whim?

"Are you mad at me, Uncle Clay?"

Franny's sad little voice interrupted his thoughts. "Of course not, muffin. I'm just thinking." He gave her a little squeeze.

"Oh. You were frowning. Are you mad at Jessie? She tooked

really good care of me." She peered anxiously into his face. "I don't want you to be mad at Jessie. She cries at night sometimes."

He smiled at her matter-of-fact tone. "She does, huh?"

Franny nodded. "I asked her one time why she was crying, and she said she missed her brother but that I made everything all better."

"That's 'cause you're a special little girl. You make everything better for me too. I didn't know Jessie had a brother."

"His name is Jasper, and he had a tadpole in his bedroom. The policeman came and took him and Jessie never saw him again." Woe was in her voice when she told him the story. "He was just a little boy. Can the policeman take me away from you and Jessie?"

"Of course not. You'll always be with me." He couldn't speak for Jessica, but the story had touched his heart when Ellen told him about it before she died. Could Jasper still be alive?

They reached the boardwalk, so he set her down and took her hand. "Are you hungry?"

"Uh-huh. Can I have some chicken?"

"Chicken it is."

The restaurant was filled with the appetizing aromas of fried chicken, beef roast, coffee, and bread. Clay's mouth watered when a waitress went by with plates of fried chicken. It sounded good to him too. He found a table near the window and ordered chicken for both of them, then turned to look around the room.

Several soldiers waved to him and a couple stopped by his table to welcome him back to the fort. The place was mostly filled with miners and soldiers, but he caught an occasional glimpse of an emigrant family. The waitress had just brought them their food when Jessica came in the door accompanied by a man of about forty-five. He had dark hair with wings of gray, and he seemed very attentive to Jessica.

The noise in the hotel stilled as the other men stared at her, too, but she seemed oblivious to the attention. *She's probably used to it.* A woman with her beauty was used to being ogled and cosseted wherever she went. That was probably another reason this past month had been so hard for her. Maybe he was expecting too much from her. How did he expect her to suddenly change who she was overnight?

He was surprised by the jealousy that burned in his chest. He felt a shaft of panic. When had he begun to care about her? He thought back to the kiss they had shared just before Ellen's death. Jessica's lips had been soft and pliant under his own, and she'd not shown the experience he expected. His pulse raced at the memory, and he determinedly stared down at his plate. He couldn't let his feelings get the best of him. She wasn't a Christian.

As he ate his supper, he tried to pay attention to Franny's chatter, but his eyes kept straying to Jessica's red curls. She talked animatedly with the man, who kept his gaze fastened on her face. The fellow was obviously smitten. Jessica threw back her head and laughed. Her melodious laughter made other heads turn. Even Franny turned around in her seat at the familiar sound.

"It's Jessie!" She slid from her chair and evaded Clay's restraining hand. "Jessie!"

Jessica turned at the sound and opened her arms. Her face lit up at the sight of Franny. *She really does love her.* He'd never been totally sure of her motives before, but the adoration on her face was obvious. Franny hurtled into her arms, and Jessica kissed her, while the man looked on with an indulgent smile. It was a proprietary smile, as though he were looking at his own wife and child. Maybe that's what Jessica and Franny needed: stability with someone who could provide for them. Did he have the right to deny them that?

He rose slowly to his feet and sauntered toward the other table. "Sorry, I couldn't stop her when she realized you were here."

Jessica gazed up at him with a look on her face that made his heart leap. It almost seemed like the same look she gave Franny. *Stop it!* She was a master at making men fall in love with her. She played with men's hearts like men played with cards. He needed to keep her character well in mind. "Enjoying your supper?"

"Very much." Her companion stood, and she smiled at him. "I'd like you to meet Robert Ketcham. Robert, this is Franny's cousin and co-guardian, Reverend Clay Cole."

Clay shook the man's hand and was impressed with his direct gaze and firm shake. He wanted to find a reason to dislike him, but if first impressions were anything to go by, he wouldn't find a thing wrong with the other man.

"Please join us." Robert gestured at the two empty seats. "We were just about to enjoy a piece of Martha's famous apple pie."

Clay wanted to refuse, but he also didn't want to seem churlish. He smiled his thanks and took Franny from Jessica, then placed her on a chair and scooted her up to the table before sitting down across from Robert. He might as well find out as much as possible about the situation while he was here.

"What do you do?" he asked Robert. He listened as Robert explained his business and his desire to discover new markets and horizons. He seemed like a nice guy. Clay didn't want to like him, but he couldn't help himself.

As soon as their pie was finished, Clay took his leave and left Franny with Jessica. She was heading back to the cabin, and he needed to get away somewhere and think. He was shocked at how much the thought of Jessica being interested in another man shook him. He strolled through the dusty streets, looking up at the stars. The whine of the sawmill had ceased, and frogs croaked in the stillness.

His cabin was cold and lonely when he shut the door behind him. He lit a lantern, then started a small fire to take the edge off the chill, and looked around his cold, empty room. This was likely all his life would be: a series of empty rooms where he hung his hat for a few days or weeks before he moved on to the next place. Would the Lord ever give him a home of his own, his own family, and his own church? Did he even want that? Jessica stirred a sense of longing he'd never thought to have. He poked the fire dejectedly, then picked up his Bible. He was never alone, and he knew it. There was no sense in wallowing in self-pity.

He thumbed through the pages and found Psalm 84:10, one of his favorite verses: "For a day in thy courts is better than a thousand. I had rather be a doorkeeper in the house of my God, than to dwell in the tents of wickedness."

Instead of stopping there he read the next verse. He didn't

remember reading the verses with quite the same meaning he saw now. "For the LORD God is a sun and shield: the LORD will give grace and glory: no good thing will he withhold from them that walk uprightly."

No good thing. Did that mean a family someday, a godly wife, and a houseful of children? He closed the Bible with finality. Why was he thinking like this now? Whatever the future held, he was sure of one thing: Jessica DuBois wasn't part of it.

Robert pressed Jessica's hand and wished her a good night before slipping off into the dark night. She stood for a moment on the front stoop with Franny in her arms and listened to the crickets. It was a peaceful night, but she felt far from settled. Clay had ruined everything. One look at those broad shoulders and warm hazel eyes had shattered her resolve to leave Fort Bridger by whatever means it took. Oh, she still intended to leave with Robert if she could, but her courage was gone. It would be so much harder with Clay here. She would have to fight her feelings for him every minute as well as focus on winning Robert's affections. Of course, that deed was already well on its way to accomplishment. He had been an easy target.

She had been conscious of Clay's gaze all evening. She'd tried to act gay and uncaring, but it had all been a facade. She was so tired of playacting, tired of living up to everyone else's expectations of who and what she should be. She suddenly wanted to sit and talk with her mother, but there never seemed to be any time for just the two of them anymore. One member or the other of her mother's new family was always demanding her attention. Maybe Jessica should make more of an effort to be friendly with her cousins. She needed someone to fill this empty ache inside her.

She undressed Franny and slipped her into her nightgown, then read her the Bible verses Clay had prescribed for the night. Every night it got harder and harder to read those verses. They seemed to mock her. She could never hope to be good enough to understand what they meant. Tonight's verse was a good example, John 3:3: "Verily, verily, I say unto thee, Except a man be born again, he cannot see the kingdom of God."

She wasn't sure exactly what being born again meant, but it sounded life-changing and alarming. She hated being confronted every night by these Scriptures, but she had promised Clay to teach Franny. The problem was it was hard to explain something she didn't understand herself.

She kissed Franny good night, then went to the stove and heated some water for tea. She missed Ellen. Ellen always seemed to know what to do about everything. Jessica needed a friend. But there was no one.

She jumped when someone knocked at the door. Her heart pounded. Was it Clay? She hurried to the door and opened it. Miriam stood scowling at her. Her cousin pushed past her without a word, then glared at her with her arms folded in front of her.

"Your mother sent me to fetch you," she said abruptly.

"What's wrong?" She couldn't keep the alarm from her voice.

"We've been ranked out and have until eight o'clock tomorrow morning to get out."

"Oh no." It was a common practice in the army for a superior officer to demand a lower officer's quarters on short notice. "Where will you go? The fort is filled to capacity." Jessica's thoughts raced as she tried to think of any empty buildings or cabins she'd seen.

"That's why your mother wants to talk to you. I'm supposed to stay here with Franny."

Jessica glanced at the little girl and saw she hadn't been disturbed by the knock on the door. "All right," she said with reluctance. "I shouldn't be long. Thanks for staying."

Miriam looked surprised at the thanks but nodded.

She hurried across the parade ground. Was the tension between Miriam and her Jessica's fault? Had she been so prickly and unapproachable that the other girl had retaliated in kind? It was something to consider.

The DuBois residence was a bustle of activity when she entered. Caleb and Uncle Samuel were piling boxes and crates in the hall, while her mother and Bridie packed breakables in wooden crates filled with hay.

Her mother looked up, then burst into tears. "Jessica, you must help us!" She fluttered her hands. "We've no one else to turn to."

"What can I do, Mama? Do you want me to talk to the colonel?" It probably wouldn't help. He'd lost his interest in her since Major Adams brought his daughter to the fort.

"We need a place to stay, darling. Can we stay with you?" Jessica began to frown, and Mama hastened to add, "Just for a little while. Something else will open up soon."

"But . . . but, Mama, my cabin is tiny!" Her thoughts whirled as she tried to think where she could put all of them.

"I know, darling, but there is nowhere else for us to go." Her mother looked at her piteously and more tears trickled down her cheeks. "We can't sleep on the streets."

Uncle Samuel cleared his throat gruffly. "Your mother is right. I've searched high and low for a place for us. It's either your cabin or a tent."

Jessica couldn't imagine her mother in a tent. "Of course you can stay. But I have no idea where we can put your things."

"I've already thought about that," Uncle Samuel said. "I've arranged for some tents for the majority of our things. We'll set up camp outside your back door for easy access to our possessions. All we'll bring inside are the beds and necessities."

"That should work." She still was uncertain about it. The freedom of her own place was one of her only compensations for her new life. Now she would have to put up with Miriam, but it would be good to have her mother close.

Her uncle didn't wait for her to change her mind. "Caleb, come with me and we'll see about setting up the tents. Bridie, you go spell Miriam with little Franny and let Miriam help Letty with the packing for a while. Once the tents are set up, Caleb and I will bring the beds over. Jessica, you rearrange your things to find room for us and we'll be over soon."

She bristled at his order but said nothing. She knew he was right. But if he thought he would talk to her like that all the time, he would find out he was wrong. She sighed again and went to make room for her unwelcome visitors.

Nine

The tiny cabin was packed with beds and people. Clothing hung from nails on nearly every available bit of wall space. A three-quarter-size bed was pushed into one corner for Bridie and Miriam to sleep on, a small cot for Caleb crouched behind the front door, and Uncle Samuel's four-poster bed hid behind a makeshift screen in the corner farthest from the door. Jessica had taken down Franny's cot, since the little girl slept with her much of the time anyway. Their bed was repositioned along the wall by the bed for Bridie and Miriam. There was barely enough room to walk around all the beds.

Franny had awakened during the commotion of moving but soon fell back to sleep when everything settled down. No one else had slept much, though. Breakfast had been a fiasco with everyone cross and irritated with one another. She held her tongue, though. They were all tired. She didn't want to add to her mother's burden.

After breakfast Jessica stood and tied her hair back in a kerchief. "I'd better get to work. Bridie, would you help Franny with her lessons this morning?"

Bridie looked up in surprise, but she didn't object. "Where are her books?"

Jessica sighed. "I have no idea. The last time I saw them, they were under her cot, but I don't remember where we moved them last night when we took the cot down. She'll help you find them." She looked around at the rest of the family. "Anyone want to help with the laundry?"

Miriam sniffed, her nose wrinkling. "Not me. I'm meeting my friends at the millinery shop about ten."

Her father frowned. "I think not, young lady. Your mother will need your help to get all this stuff sorted out."

"She's *not* my mother. She's my aunt." Miriam scowled.

Jessica's mother fluttered her hands. "That's fine, Samuel," she murmured. "I can get things done by myself."

Jessica's simmering temper boiled over. "Mama, there is no reason you have to do everything by yourself. Everyone lives together, and everyone needs to share in the responsibility." She shoved boxes out to the middle of the floor. "Miriam, you start unpacking these boxes. Caleb, get some money from your father and run to the sutler's store for more flour and any other supplies Mama thinks we need." She turned to Bridie. "We'll forget Franny's lessons for today. I wasn't thinking about just how much needed to be done."

Miriam put her hands on her hips and tossed her hair. "You can't tell me what to do. You unpack the boxes yourself."

"Fine," Jessica said sweetly. "You do the men's laundry, then."

Miriam stared at her for a moment, then turned and began to empty the nearest box with angry, jerky motions.

Uncle Samuel cocked an eyebrow. "Changing your tune a bit, aren't you, missy? Where were you when your mother and cousins were doing everything without your help?"

Jessica shrugged. "We were living under your roof then, but now we're under mine. I've realized how hard a household is to run. I've grown up some, I guess."

"It's about time." He turned and went toward the back door.

Jessica flushed hotly at the reprimand. "You've got a lot of nerve criticizing me when you married my mother just to have a servant. Why don't you try treating her like a wife for a change?"

Her uncle turned scarlet, but she didn't wait for a response. She had work to do. Her back stiff, she slammed the door behind her and went to the laundry tent.

She had just hung up her first load of laundry when Clay strolled up. Her mouth grew dry at the sight of his broad shoulders.

"Hey, Red, what's going on at your place?" He took off his hat and raked a hand through his dark hair.

"Mama and Uncle Samuel were ranked out last night." She turned her back to him and dumped another load of dirty clothes into the steaming tub of water. Her hands were trembling, and she hoped he didn't notice. She wished she didn't feel like this every time he was near.

He whistled softly. "Bet your uncle is madder than a bear with a sore foot. Where'd you put them all?" He put his hat back on his head and followed her when she ducked inside the tent for more soap.

She sighed. "It was hard to find room. We're all falling over one another."

"I can imagine."

His intent gaze made her flush, but hopefully he'd assume it was from the fire.

"Robert seems like a nice guy. How long have you known him?"

"What is this, an inquisition?" She brushed past him.

He held up a placating hand. "I didn't mean it to sound that way. I was just interested."

"Well, get uninterested. My relationship with Robert is my own business. You can keep your nose out of it."

His nostrils flared, but he managed to control himself.

Why was she trying to goad him into losing his temper? Was it because she wanted him to show some sort of jealousy? She almost laughed out loud at the thought. There wasn't much chance of that.

"Let's start this conversation over," he said finally. "I really just wanted to come by and see how things went with Franny while I was gone. Did you have any problems? How are you for money?"

"Fine." She softened her sharp tone. "Franny can say all the alphabet and seems to be sleeping better. She doesn't cry out for her mother in the night as much as she did." She snapped a wet sheet and hung it on the line. "As far as money goes, I'm about out, but I get my first army paycheck tomorrow. We're doing fine."

"What about her spiritual education?"

She glanced up at his anxious tone and was snared by the warm look in his eyes. She was lost in the depth of his eyes for a few long moments. Did he feel anything for her? Anything at all? She dropped her gaze.

"I've read the verses you picked out every night. Now that

you're back, we'll attend the service tomorrow." She looked up and was surprised at the look of amazed happiness on his face.

He lowered his gaze and hooded his expression. "I thought I might have to threaten and beg to get you to come."

"I'm not a complete heathen. I may have trouble believing all that stuff myself, but I want Franny to have the best of everything."

His expectant look faded. "I'll see you tomorrow then." He stepped toward her and tucked a stray curl back up into her kerchief.

Her breathing quickened at his nearness. She inhaled the clean male scent of him. For just a moment, she thought he might kiss her, but he stepped back and tipped his hat. "Sit in the front row. It will inspire me."

As he walked away her breathing returned to normal. She was determined not to let him see how much he affected her. She'd better invite Robert to attend the service with her so Clay wouldn't suspect how much she cared. She'd had all the humiliation she could take.

Clay straightened his cravat and slicked down a stray cowlick. The last few services he had held before he went to Colorado had been well attended, and he hoped this one would follow the same pattern. He was nervous about whether Jessica would really come with Franny. He wanted her to love and know his God so badly. He shied away from examining just why it was so important to him. He loved sharing God's love with people, but he wanted this for Jessica even more than usual. He tried to tell himself it was for Franny's sake, but was that the only reason?

He shook the thought away. It was probably no use anyway. He'd witnessed many times to his vain and selfish mother, who had no interest in spiritual matters at all. She'd thrown him out of the house after his last attempt, and he gathered his belongings and headed west. Every letter he'd sent her since had gone unanswered.

He clapped his hat on his head, picked up his Bible, and walked across the parade ground to the unmarried officers' quarters. The meeting room already had soldiers milling around near the door. He tipped his hat as he entered the room.

He walked up the aisle created by the benches the men had hauled in. *Please, Lord. Please let her come today. Let her hear something that creates a hunger in her heart to know and love you.*

When he looked up Jessica was coming down the aisle on Robert's arm. They seemed like a happy, prosperous family with little Franny in tow. Clay's insides clenched strangely, but he wouldn't let himself think about how he felt. He had to put those feelings behind him. They sat right in the middle of the front row, but he couldn't read Jessica's face at all this morning. She looked like the cool, self-possessed young lady he'd first met all those months ago. Perhaps it was only wishful thinking to imagine he saw a change in her.

He welcomed the worshipers to the service. As he glanced around he estimated the group at about twenty-five, a respectable showing for a busy fort like Bridger. He led the group in two hymns, then opened his Bible. "Turn to Proverbs 6:16," he told them and began to read. "'These six things doth the LORD hate:

yea, seven are an abomination unto him: a proud look, a lying tongue, and hands that shed innocent blood, an heart that deviseth wicked imaginations, feet that be swift in running to mischief, a false witness that speaketh lies, and he that soweth discord among brethren.'" Jessica's eyes widened as he read the passage.

He plunged into his sermon, and it was as though he preached to her only. As he talked of sin and forgiveness offered by God through Jesus Christ, he felt a connection with her he'd never felt with anyone before. It was almost as though he could see right into her soul to the pain and longing she had to be clean and forgiven.

Her eyes grew huge in her face, and he thought tears might be hiding there. When the service ended he tried to make his way to her, but several soldiers hurried forward to talk to him, and she left before he was finished. He rejoiced at the soldiers' responses to his message, but he was frustrated that he couldn't talk seriously with Jessica. Maybe he could catch her alone after lunch.

Jessica could barely keep her face in order following the sermon. She trembled all over but was careful to hide it from Robert and her family. She just wanted some time alone, but where could she find it? Every square inch of her cabin was filled. Her mother began to prepare lunch while Jessica got Franny out of her good dress and into her everyday one. Her mother urged Robert to stay for the meal, and he accepted quickly. Jessica was almost glad for an excuse to avoid dealing with her thoughts for a while.

After the meal Robert asked her to take a walk with him. She caught up her wrap as a barrier against the autumn wind and followed him out the door. They left the confines of the fort and followed the river past the old corral. Robert took her hand and stopped in the middle of the path.

He raised her hand to his lips and looked at her intently. "We haven't known one another very long, my dear girl, but my time here is short and I feel I must speak. I believe we would deal very well together. I could provide a good home for you and Franny." He pressed her hand ardently. "I have the highest regard for you, and I'm asking you to consider becoming my wife."

This was exactly what she'd hoped for–a man who would care for Franny and her, someone with wealth and prestige, someone kind and easygoing she could manipulate to her will. She regarded him thoughtfully.

He hastened to sweeten the deal. "I plan to build us a lovely home by the sea in San Francisco where you can entertain whenever you want. As my wife you'll be respected and revered. Please say you'll come with me."

Why was she even hesitating? She smiled at him. "Let me think about it."

He frowned. "Of course. I know this is very sudden, but surely you must have had some idea of my intentions."

"I can't say I'm surprised, but marriage is a big step."

"True. But winter will be here in a few weeks, and we must move quickly."

"Give me until tomorrow." She knew she was going to accept. It was the only solution for Franny and her, but she saw no reason to give Robert the upper hand. She must begin as she intended to go on. If she accepted his proposal, she intended to be firmly in control.

"Very well. Until tomorrow." He bent his head to kiss her, but she turned her head and his lips landed on her cheek. The touch of his lips didn't stir her as Clay's did, but she would have to learn to deal with that.

When Robert left her at her door, she couldn't bring herself to go inside the cabin. She would walk in on a scene of utter bedlam, so as soon as Robert's back disappeared from view, she cut through the yard and around the back of the cabin. A creek angled through the property, and she had always wanted to take time to follow it for a ways. Bridie would keep Franny entertained, and Jessica just needed a few minutes to herself.

The cold air whipped through her wrap. Winter came early to the mountains, and she wasn't looking forward to it. The thought of hanging clothes to dry in the frigid air was not appealing. The other laundresses didn't associate with her, or she would have asked one of them how they managed. She smiled wryly. She no longer fit in with any group. The officers' wives felt they were too good for her, and the other women thought she was above them.

The trail beside the creek suddenly petered out, and she sat on a flat rock overlooking the gurgling brook. Clay's words from his sermon came back to her mind. That Scripture he'd read about the seven things God hated had described her perfectly. She had done every single one of those things, even the shedding of blood. Although she hadn't actually killed anyone, she *had* tried to arrange Sarah Campbell's elimination. Clay had explained how such a person might be forgiven, but she didn't think it was really possible. Not for someone as uncaring about other people as she'd been.

Tears filled her eyes, and she stooped and picked up a flat stone and tossed it across the water. It skipped three times before sinking. That was just how she felt sometimes: no matter how hard she tried to keep her head above water, she always ended up sinking.

She swallowed past the tightness in her throat. Robert's offer seemed like the perfect answer, but it was really more her manipulation of events. What was it Clay said? Oh yes, something about a heart devising wicked imaginations. That's what she'd done all her life–schemed and planned to get her own way.

Suddenly the thought of leaving that kind of life behind and becoming someone with character was overwhelmingly appealing. Fear clamped her chest, and she felt like she couldn't breathe. What would it be like to turn loose the reins of her life and trust an unseen God for her future? She didn't know if she could do that. She wasn't very good at trust.

Trembling, she sank to her knees. "Oh God, I'm tired of running, tired of messing up my life. I know I've done a lot of things you hate, but I'll try to change. I want to be more like Ellen was." She could change. Once she was a better person, maybe God would forgive her.

She started back toward the cabin. A few flakes of snow drifted down, and the wind was stronger than before. She'd barely gone ten feet when the snow whipped around her and obscured her vision. Unfamiliar with the path, she stumbled over rocks and branches. Minutes later she wasn't sure where she was.

Was this a blizzard? It was only October. She drew in a ragged breath and began to run but tripped over an uprooted tree. Which way was home?

"Help!" The snow muffled her shout, and her panic rose. What if no one could hear her? The wind penetrated her wrap, and she shivered. The temperature had plummeted in the last fifteen minutes. Already the snow covered the tops of her boots. She'd never seen snow come down so fast and thick.

She was near tears when the dark outline of a building emerged ahead. She hurried toward it. She was nearly to the door when she recognized her own cabin. She let herself in the back door. Uncle Samuel was pacing the floor, her mother shook with tears, and Miriam stood sullenly in the corner.

"It's about time you got back," her uncle barked. Worry creased his forehead.

"What's happened?" Her voice rose in alarm. She glanced around the room. "Where's Franny?" Foreboding knotted in the pit of her stomach.

"Bridie took Franny for a walk, and they aren't back yet."

She pressed a hand to her throat. "I have to find Clay." He would want to be out there looking.

"Caleb went to get him." Her uncle went to the door and threw it open. "I can't even see across the parade ground! I don't know how we'll find them."

Dread rose in her throat again, but she forced it down. "Clay will find some soldiers to help search for them. I'm going too." She took her heavy coat from a nail on the wall and pulled it on. It was made of beaver and fairly warm, but the matching muff wasn't practical for the search. She wound a scarf around her throat and followed Uncle Samuel out into the driving snow. What did Franny have on? Surely it was only her thin wrap.

In the stifling white again, she was immediately disoriented. All she could do was follow her uncle's burly form and plod through the nearly knee-deep drifts. They stopped outside the corral, and Uncle Samuel shouted for his horse to be brought.

"You can't accomplish anything here. Go back with your mother. We'll find them."

She knew he was right. If she insisted on mounting a horse and following him, they would soon be searching for her as well as Bridie and Franny. She didn't know her way around the countryside well enough to be of any use in this white wilderness. She wasn't even sure she could make it back to the cabin without help. But how could she return to the warmth and safety of the cabin with Franny out here somewhere?

Uncle Samuel swung up onto his gelding, and both man and horse disappeared from view almost instantly. She turned and followed her tracks back to the cabin. New snow had already nearly filled them, so she hurried as fast as she dared. By the time she reached her cabin door, the tracks were impossible to see.

She stumbled through the doorway and all but fell into her mother's arms. The blazing fire was a welcome sight. Her mother helped her out of her coat and settled her near the fire.

"I'll get you a cup of tea, dear." She put the kettle on the stove to heat and sat beside Jessica.

"I should never have let them go," her mother fretted. "I'm so sorry, darling."

"It wasn't your fault. None of us realized this storm was blowing up. I almost didn't make it back from my walk." It did no good to blame her. "I'm the one responsible for Franny. I should have been here."

Her mother's eyes widened as she stared at her. The surprise on her face would have been comical if they weren't all so frightened.

The teakettle began to whistle, and her mother jumped up to fetch it, but Jessica restrained her. "I'll get it, Mama. You've waited on everyone today. Sit here and rest." She got to her feet and took the teakettle from the stove. She had to be a better person. Maybe then God would save Franny.

When she handed her mother a cup of tea, she could see her mother didn't know what to think of her actions. Had she really been that thoughtless and domineering that her mother would show such astonishment over a simple cup of tea? The thought was disquieting. Did anyone ever really know how others perceived them?

She took a cup across the room to Miriam. "Why don't you join us by the fire?"

Her eyes narrowed, Miriam took the proffered cup of tea. After studying Jessica's face, she grudgingly took her stool and moved it beside her aunt.

"Are you feeling all right, dear?"

"Just worried," Jessica said.

"You should be worried all the time then," Miriam sniped. "You'd be easier to live with."

Jessica was silent for a moment. "I know I've been difficult, but I've grown up some in the past few months. I hope you'll both give me another chance." It was as close as she could come to an apology right now.

"Of course," her mother said faintly.

Miriam scowled but said nothing. Her face showed her skepticism.

Jessica put her cup on the hearth and went to the door. She opened it, but the heavy snow continued to block any view of even Officers' Row across the parade ground. She was trying to cling desperately to the hope that God wouldn't allow anything to happen to Franny. Or Bridie. She'd barely spared a thought for her younger cousin. Bridie must be terrified, especially knowing she was responsible for Franny as well. If the men didn't find them soon, they would freeze.

Ten

Plodding through the snow, Clay swayed from weariness. He couldn't feel his fingers any longer, and he longed for a warm fire and dry clothes. But Franny was still out there somewhere. Even with the snow muffling everything, he would have heard a shot announcing the girls had been found.

He'd prayed and begged with all his strength for God to spare both girls, but he was beginning to lose hope. He didn't see any way they could have survived this blizzard. It would take a miracle for him to ever feel Franny's arms around his neck.

He should never have allowed Jessica to keep her. She'd been out gallivanting with Robert instead of taking care of her responsibilities. When would he learn never to trust a beautiful woman? They were all just like his mother, interested in only what pleased them.

Drifts of snow came nearly to his horse's belly in spots, and Misty had trouble breaking her way through. She was used to carrying him long hours, but this kind of weather was hard on both man and beast. The trouble was that with the heavy snowfall, the girls' bodies would be buried beneath the drifts, and they wouldn't find them until spring.

He pushed the thought away. He would look until there was no longer any hope.

He stopped near an outcropping of rock and slid to the ground. The snow came up to his knees, and he staggered around a straggly pine toward the shelter of a small cave in the rock face. Misty followed, her head down to avoid the wind. Was it possible they could have found shelter here? Hope rising in his chest, he knelt, brushed the snow from the entrance, and peered inside.

His heartbeat slowed when he saw the empty spot. Discouraged, he mounted Misty and turned her head toward the fort. The snowfall grew steadily lighter, and he could actually see the stockade ahead. He would let Misty get some rest and borrow someone else's horse for the morning.

When he dismounted he found Samuel preparing to go out again himself. "Any sign at all?"

Samuel shook his head. "Not a trace."

Neither man looked the other in the eye. Clay knew his hopelessness would show on his face. The girls had spent the entire night out in this blizzard, and he didn't see any way they could have survived. Even if they found a cave to huddle in, the mercury had fallen below zero. They surely would have frozen to death by now.

The snow had completely stopped, though. Clay asked for a fresh horse and swung into the saddle, then turned the horse's head toward the gate. Before he got more than a couple of steps, Jessica called to him.

She looked much different than she had a mere twenty-four hours ago. Her tangled hair had obviously not been combed, and her tearstained face was white. She put her hand on the horse's bridle.

"You have to find them, Clay." A sob caught in her throat.

He stared down at her. "Your concern is a little late, Jessica. Where were you when she wandered off into the snow? It's a little like Ellen's death, isn't it? You're always too busy thinking of yourself to worry about other people."

She was crying in earnest now. "I deserve everything you say to me. But please, you must keep searching. I just know she's still alive." She put a hand against her breast. "I can feel it here, in my mother's heart. You can't give up."

"Oh, I'm not giving up on Franny. But I'm giving up on you. God will have to reach you in his own time. I can't handle any more." He wheeled his horse around and took off as quickly as the drifts would allow. He only caught a glimpse of her stricken face before she turned and went back the way she'd come. She'd soon forget him, just like his mother had put him out of her life.

Sobs racked Jessica's body, and she struggled not to fall in the drifts along the parade ground. She couldn't blame Clay for giving up on her. She had been willful and headstrong, without a care in her head for what anyone else wanted. She should have been home caring for Franny instead of leaving it to Bridie to do. And his reference to Ellen hurt badly, because she knew it was true. If she hadn't fallen asleep, she could have kept Ellen from choking on her own vomit.

How could you let her die, God? It was my fault, not Ellen's. She wanted to raise her fists and scream. Staggering from both the weight of her guilt and the thick snow, she fell facedown in a huge drift. "God, why?" The wind caught her words and flung them away like so much chaff. "Take me instead. You always take the ones I love. What about me, God? Take me and spare my Franny."

The cold wet from the snow seeped through her clothing, but she welcomed the discomfort. She wanted to die, to just lie there and let the icy grip of the snow take her away from the pain here. She had never felt such despair, not even when she had lost Jasper and their mother.

"God, help me," she moaned. "I can't take any more. I want to believe in something better than this life, in Someone who loves me no matter what I do. Why is it so hard?" She sobbed again and burrowed deeper into the snowdrift. "Forgive me, Lord, forgive me."

Memories of the things she'd done and the people she'd hurt paraded through her memory. Belinda Cramer who had snubbed her at a party, and Jessica found revenge by stealing her fiancé. Richard Drewy who had the misfortune to catch her eye at eighteen. The parade went on and on, culminating in her behavior at Fort Laramie with Sarah Montgomery and again at Fort Phil Kearny with Emmie Croftner. How could a loving God forgive such terrible behavior? What were those sins again? Oh yes, a proud look, a lying tongue, hands that shed innocent blood, a heart that devises wicked imaginations, feet that run to mischief, a false witness that speaks lies, and sowing discord. She'd done them all and more.

"Can you forgive me, God? I know I'm not worthy, but Clay said Jesus took my punishment. I have nowhere else to turn, Lord. No one but you."

I am here, beloved. I have always been here, waiting for you to turn and acknowledge me.

She felt God's presence with a sense of wonder. Everything Clay had said was true. She pushed her hands into the snowdrift and levered her way out enough to sit up. After managing to get her feet under her, she brushed the wet, caked snow from her coat. She took a deep breath.

Jessica had some terrible things to face in the next few days, but she could sense the bedrock of God under her feet, holding her up. She would have to live with her guilt for not caring for Franny properly, but since God had forgiven her, maybe someday she could forgive herself.

Clay knew he'd been out of line with Jessica, but he hadn't been able to hold his temper in check. It was his own fault for allowing her to get under his skin. But no more. He was going to dig out and destroy the root of love that kept springing up in his heart. He didn't want to love a woman like her. He *would not* love her. And when he pulled little Franny's body out of the snowdrift she was lying in, it shouldn't be too hard to muster up dislike for the one responsible.

Plodding through the heavy snow, he found no sign of the missing girls. Growing more and more discouraged, by lunchtime he decided to check in at the fort. The crack of a rifle pierced the cold air, and he craned his head in the direction of the blast. Was it a signal? He rode in the direction of the shot and found three soldiers milling around a rock face about a quarter of a mile from the fort.

One of them waved to him. "Over here, Preacher! We found them!"

He braced himself to see Franny's lifeless little body, forcing himself to go forward. He reined in his horse about five feet from the men and slid to the ground, then fought his way through the drifts. The snow was piled high in this section because of the way the rock formation angled. One of the soldiers moved, and he saw Franny's blonde head. She was *standing*!

Clay ran the remaining few steps and scooped her up into his arms. Tears came to his eyes, and he let them fall unashamedly. Her face was white and pinched with the cold, but she seemed unhurt. How had she survived? He looked at Bridie. Her skirt hem was wet and dirty, and her hair hung on her shoulders in matted tangles, but they were both all right. He put an arm around her and hugged her too.

She burst into tears. "I was so scared, Clay. The storm came up so fast and then I couldn't see anything. I didn't know what to do."

"Whatever you did, it was the right thing. You kept Franny and yourself alive."

"We found a cave, but it was just so cold. We huddled together at the back, but I started feeling really strange and sleepy and not cold anymore. Then Buster showed up." She pointed at the golden retriever a few feet away. Buster belonged to the post commander and everyone loved him. "Me and Franny curled up with him. He saved our lives, I know."

"I'll find him some meat when we get back to the fort." He knelt and patted the dog. "Good boy, Buster."

Buster woofed and thrust his nose into Clay's hands. It was almost as though he knew he'd done well. Clay swallowed hard and got control of his emotions. He had been so certain the girls had died in the storm. God had to have protected them. There was no other explanation.

"Let's get you both home. You need a hot bath and some food." He swung up into the saddle, and one of the soldiers handed Franny up to him. He settled her against his chest and gave his hand to Bridie. She swung up behind him and put her arms around his waist.

The trip back to the fort seemed long. Clay was eager to get Franny to a warm place and into dry clothes. News of the rescue had already spread throughout the fort when they rode through the gate.

Jessica's face was the first thing Clay saw when he stopped at the stable. Although pale and strained, she gave a glad cry when she saw his precious bundle perched in front of him.

"Franny!" Jessica stumbled forward and held up her arms.

The little girl practically fell into her embrace. "Jessie, I waited for you and Uncle Clay to come find me. Me and Bridie was scared."

Jessica covered her face with kisses. "Sweetheart, we were so worried! Uncle Clay looked and looked for you. He looked for you all night."

Franny wound her arms around her neck and kissed her. "I missed you."

"I missed you too. Now let's get you home and into a hot bath and clean clothes." She carried her off toward the cabin.

Franny waved over Jessica's shoulder. "'Bye, Uncle Clay!"

He lifted his hand, then dropped it to his side as soon as Franny was out of sight. He would have to make other arrangements for Franny. Things couldn't go on like they were. He just didn't trust Jessica. When her own interests were at stake, she forgot everything and everyone else.

He plodded through the snow to his quarters, where he looked around the room as if seeing it for the first time. He'd never noticed before how stark and unwelcoming his tiny room was, holding only a bed, a battered stove with two pots, a rickety table he'd dragged out of the trash heap when an officer had moved on, and a chair with one leg missing that was propped up with a piece of wood. It was not a very welcoming environment for a little girl, but it would have to do. He'd see about adding a few furnishings.

What about when he was traveling? For the first time, he wondered if the Lord was telling him it was time to settle somewhere and build a ministry in one place. But where? And how did he know for sure?

He sat in his chair and spent some time in study and prayer

and listened to what God was saying. Franny was his family now, and he had a responsibility to her.

He closed his Bible and drew out his pocket watch. Nearly four o'clock. He sighed and picked up his coat. He wasn't looking forward to the coming confrontation. He didn't like hurting Jessica, but it had to be done. She had to know he couldn't let her negligence continue.

He knocked on her cabin door. How would he manage to talk to her alone? He owed her that much. Taking Franny would be humiliating enough without having her family witness it.

Miriam opened the door and smiled. "Clay, did you come to join the party?"

"Party?"

"Aunt Letty baked a cake and we're celebrating the safe recovery of Bridie and Franny. You have to join us." She took his arm and pulled him inside.

Jessica was sitting on the edge of the bed reading Franny a story. Franny's hair curled around her shoulder in shiny ringlets, and she was snuggled with her favorite blanket against Jessica's side. She looked happy and contented. They both looked up when he stomped the snow from his boots.

Jessica's smile brightened when she saw him, and Franny hopped to the floor and ran to him.

"Uncle Clay, Grandma Letty bakeded me a cake. It's chocolate. But I can't eat any till after supper. I'll share with you."

Grandma Letty. Franny was being assimilated into the DuBois family more every day. Before too long she would be calling Jessica Mama. He had better do something now. He looked at Jessica. "Can we talk?"

Her smile faded, and she seemed apprehensive. "Of course."

"Not here. Would you care to join me for dinner at Bridger Inn?"

"What about Franny's party?"

"We'll be back in about an hour."

Her gaze probed his face, then she nodded. "I'll tell Mama and get my coat."

While she explained to Letty, he told Franny they were going out for a bit but would be back in time to share her chocolate cake. The little girl wanted to come with them, but he promised her a licorice stick if she was good.

The only sound as they walked to the hotel was the crunch of their boots in the snow. Clay wanted to wait until they were seated to tell her his decision. Jessica kept her head down as she tried to keep up with him. He realized he was going too fast and slowed his steps.

It was early yet for the hotel supper crowd, so they were able to be seated in a corner table away from other customers. Jessica slipped off her coat, and he hung it up on the hook behind her chair, then sat across from her. She folded her hands in her lap, her blue eyes fixed on his face as she waited.

He had to admit she looked lovely tonight. Her red hair was up in a mass of curls with a few escaping to caress the smooth skin of her neck and cheeks. It was too bad she wasn't the angel she looked on the outside. Clay clenched his jaw. *Get on with it. Waiting is not going to make it any easier.*

He took a deep breath. "I've been doing a lot of thinking since last night."

"So have I," she said softly. "About more than you know."

"Ellen expected me to take care of her daughter. I've neglected that responsibility and palmed it off on you. I can't do that any longer."

"What do you mean? You haven't asked me to do anything. I asked for Franny." Her voice rose a bit.

Ignoring the alarm in her tone, he went on. "I'm going to have to cancel our arrangement. I'm taking Franny to live with me."

"But we agreed this was best for Franny." She gripped the edge of the table and leaned forward. "She needs a mother. You can't just rip her away from me. She loves me, and I love her." Her lips trembled, and tears pooled in her eyes.

It took all his resolve not to back down. "It's really too much for you."

"You think I neglect Franny?" Fire sparked in her eyes, and she started to rise from her chair but sank back down with an obvious effort at control.

"You can't just have someone else watch her every time you want to flirt with a man."

"Is that what this is all about? You're angry because Bridie watched her while I went for a walk? Robert had already brought me home, then I went for a walk alone. I wanted to think."

Was that really what was bugging him? That Jessica was seeing another man? He hated to think he might be that petty. "I just don't think you realize what a responsibility raising a child is. I think she needs to be with me. You're trying, and I can see that, but I want Franny to have a firm spiritual foundation. Almost losing her made me realize how vital it is that she know and understand about God. Life is precarious. I couldn't live with myself if someday Franny slipped away into eternity without Jesus. Right now she's too young to totally understand, but it won't be long before she'll be able to choose to follow Christ or the world. It's better to wean her away from you before she gets any more attached."

The tears finally spilled over onto her cheeks. "Please, Clay, you can't take Franny. It would be devastating to her. Give me one more chance."

"You'll marry and have your own children. Franny would just be in the way."

The waitress brought their food, and they both fell silent. Jessica kept her gaze down and chewed on her lip. As soon as the waitress walked away, she began again.

"Give me just until Christmas. You said you had to get to three other forts by Christmas. Finish your trips, and we'll reevaluate at the beginning of next year."

He hardened his heart against her entreaty. "I've made up my mind, and there's nothing you can say to persuade me differently."

Fresh tears poured from her eyes, and she jumped to her feet. "I won't let you! You can't take her away!" She grabbed her coat and ran from the dining room. The other diners stared, then went back to their meals. Clay threw his money on the table and grabbed his coat too. Suddenly he wasn't very hungry.

Jessica sobbed as she hurried across the parade ground. Tears of both anger and pain. How could Clay do this to her or to Franny? Didn't he understand how traumatic it would be? And how could he take Franny into danger when he traveled? He'd have to find someone to care for her, and there was no one else to do it but Jessica.

Could she ask the colonel to intervene? But he had no real authority over Clay. Would he listen to Robert? As soon as the thought struck her, she discarded it. In spite of what Clay had said, her relationship with Robert was how this all began. He might say he thought Robert was a good man, but she doubted he really believed it. Could he be jealous? Did he care anything about her at all? He was just too hard to read.

She had gotten control of her emotions by the time she got back home. Franny looked up with a bright smile when she came in.

"Where's Uncle Clay? He promised to come for my party."

"He'll probably be here soon." Would he insist on taking Franny tonight? She gave herself a mental shake. He wouldn't want to upset her right after her ordeal in the blizzard. Perhaps she could think of something in the next few hours to change his mind. She couldn't give up Franny.

Clay showed up for a few minutes and ate a piece of cake with Franny. When he finished, he asked Jessica to walk him to the door. A ball of dread formed in her stomach, but she followed him to the door.

"You need to tell her tomorrow," he said. "I'll pick her up tomorrow night. I have a few things to do to get ready for her."

"Please don't do this, Clay," she whispered.

His jaw tightened. "I am sorry, Red. Someday you'll see this was for the best."

The funny thing was, she believed he was sincere. She couldn't fault him for not loving Franny. She knew what kind of man he was. He wouldn't be doing this if he wasn't totally convinced it was best. But there had to be a way to convince him he was wrong. She stared into his eyes and saw no reason to hope. She struggled not to cry, to beg, but the only way she could hold her tongue was to walk away and let him see himself out.

She lay awake long into the night considering her options. She could let Franny go without raising any more arguments. She could go to the commander and hope he could change Clay's mind. She could marry Robert and ask him to leave tomorrow with her and Franny before Clay could find out and stop them. The last option held the most appeal. It would be just what he deserved for his pigheaded refusal to see reason. She and Franny would have a good life with Robert.

Trust me.

Her eyes widened. Trust God with something this important? Where had that idea come from? How could she just sit back and do nothing? What if he didn't have the same idea about what was best as she did?

Trust me.

The persuasion to do just that tugged at her again. This was a chance to put her new faith to the test. If God proved his faithfulness in something so important to her, he could be trusted with anything. But did she really believe that? How could she go about finding the courage to take her hands off the situation and leave it in God's hands?

"God, help me," she whispered. "Help me to trust you enough to allow you to work. I don't know if I have enough faith."

She would do it. She would tell Robert she couldn't marry him. Once that safeguard was removed, she would have no one to depend on but God. She would have to trust him. A sense of peace stole over her, and she finally fell asleep, but her dreams were haunted by images of Franny clinging to her in tears.

When she awoke, her mother was already banging pots at the stove. Franny still slept, and Jessica breathed a sigh of relief. She wanted to tell her mother what was happening first and ask her to help. She slid out of bed and slipped behind the makeshift screen to wash and dress. When she emerged, she was determined to hold to her resolve from the night before. With God's help, she would hold her temper in check, allow Clay to take Franny, continue her work as laundress, and stand back to see God at work. It would be the hardest thing she had ever done.

Eleven

Clay had managed to obtain a cot for Franny from Mrs. Captain Berry and some pots from the quartermaster, and he had bought some extra supplies from the sutler's store. He set the cot up in a corner of his room and roped off a partition around it with an old blanket. Mrs. Berry had also given him a flat but still serviceable pillow and a faded pink quilt he spread over the bed. The little "room" looked welcoming with a gingham-covered barrel sitting beside the cot as a washstand. He put a battered trunk at the foot of the bed for Franny's clothes, and on the floor beside the bed he threw a hooked rug he'd bought from an emigrant family passing through Bridger. Not a bad day's work. He hoped Franny would like it.

At six o'clock he made a final inspection, then grabbed his coat and headed toward Suds Row. At least Jessica wouldn't have to wash clothes anymore. She could marry her rich suitor and go off to a life of leisure. He had been out of his mind to try to change her.

The door was opened almost immediately at his knock. He had expected to find Jessica and Franny both in tears, but Jessica was smiling when she opened the door.

"You're a bit late," she said cheerfully. "Franny was beginning to fret."

Had she told Franny yet? Did she think he'd changed his mind?

Franny squealed and ran to him. "Uncle Clay, Jessie said I get to stay with you for a little bit."

He picked her up and kissed her. "I'm real excited about it too."

She patted his face. "I'll try not to let you be sad. Mommy and Daddy are in heaven together. They aren't sad, and Jessie says we shouldn't be too sad either. We can miss them, but we should be happy they are with Jesus. That's what Jessie says."

His mouth dropped open, and he quickly shut it. He shot a glance at Jessica, but she just looked serenely back. "Jessie said that?"

Franny nodded. "Jessie is going to learn me to read in the evenings after she's done working. I told her she could stay for supper sometimes. She can, can't she, Uncle Clay?"

He heard the anxiety in her voice and hastily reassured her. "Jessie can come and see us anytime she wants."

"And I can spend the night with her sometimes, and she can sleep over with me sometimes."

He wanted to laugh but kept his face sober. "Well, you can spend the night with her sometimes."

Franny frowned, but before she could argue, Jessica interrupted. "You'll want to come stay here so you can see Bridie and feed Buster."

The little girl nodded vigorously.

"Her things are all ready," Jessica said before Franny could come up with anything else.

Franny was delighted with her "room." She put Molly on the faded pink quilt and helped Jessica pack her clothes away in the trunk. Clay was astonished at how easily the transition was accomplished. Jessica must have handled the explanation very well. He had to admit that he was surprised by how amenable she had been. He'd expected another argument at least, and maybe a downright screaming fit. Something was different about her, but he couldn't put his finger on what it was.

Jessica kissed Franny good-bye, then quickly left, but not before Clay saw tears in her eyes. She had been braver than he ever would have believed.

The next morning he took Franny with him and went to see Colonel Edwards. The post commander's office was empty of support staff, an unusual occurrence for which he was glad.

Colonel Edwards rose when he saw Clay. "Preacher! I haven't seen you in a while. How long are you in town for?" He indicated for Clay to have a seat. "Franny, would you like a licorice stick?" Anticipating her response, he was already reaching for one in the glass container on his desk. "What can I do for you, Preacher?"

"Circumstances have changed a bit for me, Colonel, and I need your help."

Colonel Edwards leaned back in his chair. "Shoot."

"I would like to establish a church here at Fort Bridger. A real church, not just services that meet in the officers' quarters. Fort Bridger is becoming a stopping-off place and is growing fast. We need to have a spiritual base before immorality and drunkenness get out of hand. I'd like some help getting a spot and having a building erected." This was a subject close to the commander's heart, Clay knew. He'd asked Clay to consider making his home here several months ago.

"That's wonderful news, my boy. I've had a spot in mind for some time now. It's at the end of the main commercial district, and it should prove to be a good location for discouraging the drunken carousing from the bars. Let me show you what I have in mind." He rose, grabbed his coat, and led the way out the door.

Clay was impressed with the site. Before he and the commander parted, Colonel Edwards had promised to put some men on construction right away. Clay walked away with a sense of peace that he was following the Lord's leading. He had asked the Lord for an open door if this was what he wanted, and it wasn't just cracked open, it was wide open. Clay would be able to create a stable home for Franny as well as minister to those traveling through on their way west.

When he and Franny stopped at Bridger Inn for lunch, he saw Robert eating alone at a table. Clay hesitated, then walked back to see him.

Robert looked up and pointed to the other chairs. "Join me."

Clay sat Franny down on a chair and dropped into the one beside her. "When are you and Jessica leaving?"

Robert looked at him blankly. "What are you talking about? I'm leaving tomorrow morning, but Jessica isn't coming with me."

"I didn't know," Clay said lamely, unable to stem the tide of relief that washed over him. She wasn't marrying Robert. He forced down his elation. It changed nothing. She was still the same person, self-centered and willful. He wished she could be different, that he could be free to love her, but it was not to be.

Clay prayed over the food, and as they ate their lunch, Clay had an opportunity to talk to Robert about the state of his soul. Robert promised to think about it.

As they parted Robert shook his hand. "Take good care of her."

Clay looked down and put his hand on Franny's golden curls. "I will."

"I mean Jessica," Robert corrected. "She's more fragile than she seems."

Clay's gaze met that of the other man. "Things will sort themselves out."

"She loves you, you know."

Shock rippled through Clay. Jessica loved him? He frowned. Had she told Robert a lie to get out of going with him?

Robert answered his unspoken question. "She didn't tell me, but it was obvious. You must be blind if you can't see it." His face red, he cleared his throat with a cough. "Take care, Preacher. Pray for me sometimes." He gave a small wave and stepped out into the melting snow.

Clay was still in shock. What made Robert think Jessica loved him? Could it be possible? He shook his head. Robert had to be just rationalizing Jessica's rejection of his proposal.

Jessica pushed the hair from her face and thrust her hands back into the hot water. Only two more pairs of pants and she was done for the day. She missed Franny's chatter with a fierce ache. The past two weeks had seemed interminably long.

One good thing had come from the storm's enforced togetherness: she had finally seen that most of the fault with her cousins had been on her side. The Lord opened her eyes to her attitudes, and she softened her tone to Miriam. Miriam began to respond, just as Jessica had once responded to Ellen. With time, Jessica felt she might be able to share her faith with her cousin.

Her uncle had even seemed to be kinder to her mother. She wasn't sure if he had actually taken a look at himself after their sharp disagreement the morning they were ranked out, but he had told her mother he would begin to look for a striker to help once they got in quarters of their own again. The pinched look around her mother's eyes had eased, and she looked almost happy lately.

Jessica still saw Franny three nights a week and taught her lessons, and last weekend Clay had allowed Franny to spend the night on Saturday. Jessica could only continue to bring her pain to God, trusting that he would somehow work everything out.

She still hadn't told anyone that she had accepted Christ. She wanted them to see a difference in her and ask if she had become a Christian. She'd gotten some strange looks, but so far no one had asked.

Jessica hung the last pair of pants up to dry and dumped out her water. Her hands throbbed like a sore tooth. The cold coupled with the soap and water had left them cracked and bleeding. She put a bleeding knuckle in her mouth and dashed through the rain from the tent to the cabin. It had rained for three days now. First the weather had warmed enough to melt the snow and then the rain had started. She was heartily sick of waking to gray, dreary skies every day.

Her second paycheck came last week, and she had considered catching a stage to Boston, but she just couldn't leave Franny. It would be like leaving part of herself behind, so she had grimly continued on with her duties. She was determined to stick it out until God showed her another direction. He seemed to want her here, and here she would stay as long as she had breath and courage left. It was already nearly Thanksgiving, and she thanked God daily that he had helped her make it this far.

She put a kettle on the stove to boil water for tea, chilled to the bone from the damp. The sound of several shouts outside made her turn, and when the shouts changed to screams, she ran and threw open the door. The sight that greeted her made her stagger back.

A wall of water roared down the swollen river that ran through the middle of the parade ground. She saw Lieutenant Sanders clinging to a splintered piece of tree before the roaring wave carried him from her sight. Barrels and household goods were carried along by the crest of the water and on past her. When the wave passed, the water lapped at her doorstep and rushed down the sides of the cabin. *The back door!*

She slammed the front door shut and raced to the back, but when she threw the door open, frigid water gushed across the threshold and over her boots. No way out there. She slammed the door shut and went to the front door again. She had to get to Franny!

She grabbed her shawl and opened the door again. Water rushed in, and before she could move, it was up to her ankles, encasing her legs in freezing cold. She waded out onto the stoop and across the yard. The water was cold, and soon its icy grip lapped at her knees. The current made it hard to keep to her feet. Someone shouted her name and she turned.

Clay waved to her from a small boat. "Stay there! I'll come get you!"

"Franny?"

"Safe!"

Swaying from the fierce current, she nodded and waited for him to reach her. She saw a movement out of the corner of her eye and turned to look. Miriam, her eyes wide with terror, swept past her on the crest of a fresh wave. Miriam screamed, then her head slammed against an uprooted tree. Her eyes closed, and her head sank beneath the waves.

"No!" Jessica dove into the waves and the cold water nearly took her breath away. She frantically swam toward her cousin. "Hold on, Miriam!" She had to get to her. Her cousin wasn't ready to face eternity yet.

Miriam's body tumbled with the rest of the flotsam in the flood. Her head went underwater and she floated limply, then another wave tumbled her again and she turned faceup, her eyes closed. A barrel surged by and Jessica grabbed it. Kicking her feet, she used it as a float and managed to get to Miriam's side. Holding one arm around the barrel, Jessica tried to reach her. Her fingers stretched as far as she could, but Miriam's sleeve evaded her. She tried again, leaning out as far as she dared without losing her grasp on the barrel.

"God, help me!" An infinitesimal stretch farther, and she snagged Miriam's sleeve. Quickly she pulled her toward the barrel. Was she dead? Jessica drew her against her chest and held on until Clay could come.

Where was he? She sobbed with the effort of hanging on to Miriam's dead weight. Just when she thought she couldn't hold on a moment longer, strong arms grabbed hold of her.

"I've got you, Red." He guided her hands to the side of the boat. "Hold on while I get Miriam in the boat."

He seized Miriam and dragged her into the boat, then lifted Jessica free of the frigid water and pulled her to safety. He threw a blanket over her, and she huddled into it gratefully. She coughed up the water she'd inhaled as she looked down at Miriam lying on the bottom of the boat. Her eyes were still closed, and blood ran from a cut on her forehead, but her chest rose and fell with her breathing. She was alive.

The boat bumped the shore, and Clay quickly tied it off to a tree so it wasn't at the mercy of the roaring floodwaters. "We'll wait here until we can get some help."

She looked up and met Clay's anxious eyes. As their gazes locked, her breath caught in her throat. Surely that was love she saw blazing there. She reached up to touch his face with a trembling hand.

He caught her hand and kissed her palm. "What's happened to you? The old Jessica would never have risked her life for someone else."

"Jesus found me."

"You've become a Christian without telling me," he whispered.

"I saw how much you'd changed, but I was afraid to hope it meant anything but willful determination." His thumb traced the contours of her lip. "Why didn't you tell me?"

"I wanted you to notice by yourself. I told God it was in his hands, and he would have to work it out." She leaned her cheek into his palm. "I wanted what you had. You and Ellen."

"I love you, you know." He put his other hand against the other side of her face and leaned forward. His lips touched hers, and the warmth drove the last remnants of the cold from her limbs. Leaning into his embrace, she gave a sob and lurched forward, nearly tipping the boat.

Miriam opened her eyes. "I may have looked as cold as a wagon tire, but I'm very much alive. While I'm grateful you saved my life, Jessica, I've played dead all I'm going to. Will you two get on with the marriage proposal before we end up in the drink again?"

Clay grinned, and Jessica made a noise that was half sob and half laugh. "Guess we'd better make Franny a happy girl and give her the mama she wants. You game, Red?"

She put her hands around his face and kissed him very deliberately. "Just try to get away now."

Epilogue

January 19, 1868

Her wedding day. They'd had to wait until another preacher could make it to Bridger to marry them, or they would have been wed already. As it was, the delay had allowed the men to throw up the small church building, so they actually had a real church to be married in. It had also given her time to write to Sarah Campbell and Emmie Liddle. She had wanted to thank them for their prayers and tell them about accepting Christ. Although they had been unable to come to the wedding, she had received warm letters from both of them.

Miriam fluffed her hair and grumbled. "No one will notice me with you in the room."

"I'm the bride. It's supposed to be that way."

"I suppose." Miriam turned and looked toward the door. "What's keeping Clay?"

Jessica frowned. "I don't know. He said he was picking up a wedding gift for me." She sighed. "Silly man. I told him I was getting all I wanted with him and Franny."

Outside the door the wedding music started up. "He must be back. Do I look all right?" Jessica pulled the veil over her face and adjusted it quickly.

"You'd put an angel to shame. Let's go." Her cousin opened the door for Jessica and followed her out the door.

The seats were packed in the small church. Jessica smiled at her mother as she passed her, then fixed her eyes to the front of the church where the man she loved waited. Reverend Slagel, his bald head shining in the light, stood to the left of Clay. Another man stood beside him, but Jessica didn't pay any attention to either one of them. She drank in the sight of Clay in his black suit, his marrying and burying suit, only now he was the one getting married. She suppressed a smile. She was almost to his side when she spared a glance at the stranger.

Red-haired and freckled, the man looked vaguely familiar. Then he smiled at her, and she saw the small gap between his front teeth. She stopped short in the aisle. With a trembling hand she raised her veil and stared.

"Sissy." He took a step toward her and smiled that gap-toothed smile again.

"Jasper?" She took a step closer. "Jasper!" With a cry she threw herself into his waiting arms and burst into tears. "Is it really you?"

The entire congregation stood, clapping and cheering. Tears poured down her cheeks. Was this real? If it was a dream, she didn't ever want to wake up. Jasper released her and Clay took her in his arms, and she buried her face in his chest. "How . . . where . . . ?"

He grinned and kissed her tenderly. "God helped," was all he said.

Jessica finally composed herself and gazed into the smiling eyes of the most wonderful man in the world. With a deep breath she put her hand in his and raised her expectant gaze to the preacher.

Love had called, and her heart had finally answered.

Discussion Questions

1. Why do you think some people need more attention than others?
2. Why do we tend to instantly judge other people by appearances?
3. Have you ever had a relationship that changed you the way Ellen influenced Jessica?
4. We never really know how our actions will reverberate with other people. Ellen died never really knowing she'd changed Jessica. Is there a relationship you have where you keep doing your best but you're not sure you're having any impact?
5. Clay was determined not to get involved with a non-Christian. Have you ever been negatively influenced by another person?
6. Children often bring out the best in people. Why do you think that happens?
7. What experience do you think changed Jessica the most?
8. What was your favorite part of the novel?

Acknowledgments

I'm so blessed to belong to the terrific HarperCollins Christian Publishing dream team! I've been with my great fiction team for fourteen years, and they are like family to me. I learn something new with every book which makes writing so much fun for me!

Our fiction publisher, Daisy Hutton, is a gale-force wind of fresh air. She thinks outside the box, and I love the way she empowers me and my team. The last two books have been with my terrific editor, Amanda Bostic, who really gets suspense and has been my friend from the moment I met her all those years ago. Fabulous cover guru Kristen Ibgebretson works hard to create the perfect cover—and does. And, of course, I can't forget the other friends in my amazing fiction family: Becky Monds, Becky Philpott, Kristen Golden, Karli Jackson, Samantha Buck, Paul Fisher, and Stephen Tindal. You are all such a big part of my life. I wish I could name all the great folks at HCCP who work on selling my books through different venues. I'm truly blessed!

Julee Schwarzburg is a dream editor to work with. She totally gets romantic suspense, and our partnership is pure joy.

She brought some terrific ideas to the table with this book—as always!

My agent, Karen Solem, has helped shape my career in many ways, and that includes kicking an idea to the curb when necessary. We are about to celebrate fifteen years together! And my critique partner of seventeen years, Denise Hunter, is the best sounding board ever. Thanks, friends!

I'm so grateful for my husband, Dave, who carts me around from city to city, washes towels, and chases down dinner without complaint. My kids—Dave, Kara (and now Donna and Mark)— love and support me in every way possible, and my little granddaughter Alexa makes every day a joy. She's talking like a grown-up now, and having her spend the night is more fun than I can tell you.

Most important, I give my thanks to God, who has opened such amazing doors for me and makes the journey a golden one.

About the Author

Photo by Clik Chick Photography

Colleen Coble is a *USA Today* bestselling author and RITA finalist best known for her romantic suspense novels, including *Tidewater Inn*, *Rosemary Cottage*, and the Mercy Falls, Lonestar, and Rock Harbor series.

Visit her website at www.colleencoble.com

Twitter: @colleencoble

Facebook: colleencoblebooks

Enjoy an excerpt from Colleen Coble's

To Love a Stranger, available July 2016

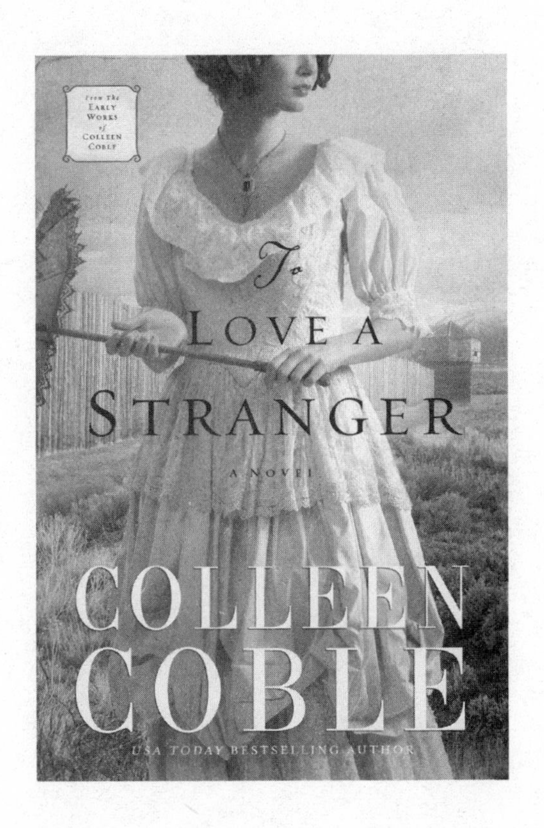

Prologue

April 1868

Fort Bridger, Utah Territory

"You are not going to marry some chit you've never set eyes on, Jasper! I don't care what kind of promise you made."

Jasper Mendenhall winced at the strident tone in his sister's voice. Still, he was glad to hear her say his name in any kind of voice. Just a few months ago he was certain he had no hope of ever seeing her again. Sent to different homes from the orphanage, their reunion had seemed a lost dream. But now at long last they had found each other.

He glanced at Jessie. Her face had flushed bright with the intensity of her emotions and nearly matched her red hair. He resisted the urge to tell her to mind her own business. She was just showing sisterly apprehension, but it still grated a bit. He wasn't some callow youth. "I know her quite well, Jessie. We've been corresponding for over six months. I appreciate your concern, but I must ask you to stay out of this."

Clay Cole put a restraining hand on her arm. "Calm down, sweetheart. It's not good for the baby for you to get upset." He guided his wife to a nearby chair. Once she was seated he turned to Jasper. "I can't say I'm in favor of this idea either. What do you really know about this woman? She could say anything in a letter. What is her name again?"

"Bessie. Bessie Randall. She's twenty-six and lives in Boston."

Jessica sniffed and wrinkled her nose. "Huh! A spinster. She's probably homely as a fishwife, Jasper."

He took a picture from the pocket of his blue uniform jacket. "See for yourself." He handed the picture to Clay, who glanced at it, then gave it to Jessica.

She stared at it and sniffed again. "All right, she's beautiful, and that makes it even worse. How can you even contemplate taking a lovely young woman out to the Arizona Territory? She looks refined and gently reared. Have you even told her what kind of conditions she'll be facing at Fort Bowie? Besides, something must be wrong with her if she's so beautiful and still unmarried. That pretty face probably hides a shrew."

Jasper and Clay looked at one another and grinned.

Jessica's flushed cheeks darkened even more, and she had the grace to look embarrassed. "I can see what you're thinking. And if it was once true in my case, that just goes to prove what I was saying. Now answer my question. Did you tell her where you'll be stationed?"

Jasper shifted his gaze from her accusing glare. He hadn't told Bessie everything. He wanted to surprise her. He knew her well enough from her letters to know she craved adventure and would welcome the challenge. But what if Jessica was right? Was it proper to take his beloved to such a wild and untamed place?

"I thought not." Jessica's voice held a trace of satisfaction. "Jasper, think about this before you do it. You should wait until you find the right woman. I want you to have what Clay and I have. Don't settle for second best." She sent a tender glance toward Clay, and he smiled back just as tenderly.

Jasper wanted what they had too. And he was certain he and Bessie would have that, given time. He already loved her fire and spirit, the tenderness he found in her letters. He longed for a home and children. "It's already done, Jessie."

Clay and Jessica both looked at him sharply. He shrugged and turned his head. They might as well hear it all. "She went through a proxy marriage and sent me the papers. I did the same and sent her the marriage lines and tickets last week. She's my wife, and I expect you to make her welcome when she gets here. She should be here within the month." He said the last firmly. Jessica could still be a bit of a termagant if she thought someone was taking advantage of her precious family.

She rose to her feet and stared at him. The color drained out of her face. "Jasper, what have you done?"

One

April 1868

Boston, Massachusetts

"What are you doing in my room, Bessie?"

Bessie Randall heard Lenore's shrill voice as though from a great distance. The lines of writing wavered before her eyes, and the hand that held the letter shook violently. This letter couldn't mean what it said. It just wasn't possible. She stared at the words again, then closed her eyes briefly before turning to face her sister.

She held out the letter. "What is the meaning of this, Lenore?"

Lenore's pale, lovely skin flushed. She shifted her gaze guiltily and swallowed hard. "What are you doing going through my things?" Her tone of outrage didn't ring true. Her blue eyes filled with tears, and she bit her lip.

"Don't try to change the subject. I was looking for my ostrich fan you borrowed for church last week." Bessie waved the letter in the air. "And it's a good thing I did. I never would have known about this." She desperately hoped there was some explanation other than the obvious.

Lenore gulped. "It's rather difficult to explain." She wound a raven lock around her finger and avoided Bessie's gaze.

"I should say so! There seems to be train and stage tickets here with the letter too. Tickets to Fort Bridger, Utah Territory–in *my* name." Bessie let out an incredulous laugh. Utah Territory! That was the last place she would want to go. She had heard about the Indian uprisings and bloodshed out there.

"If you would just let me explain." Lenore implored her with a pleading glance. "It started so innocently." She took a deep breath, then blurted it all out. "Jasper Mendenhall sent a letter to Marjorie's agency six months ago. I had just started volunteering there, and it seemed so romantic to help lonely bachelors in the West find mates. Jasper wanted to correspond with a young woman interested in marriage. I saw his picture and was quite taken with him."

Bessie took several deep breaths. It wouldn't do to get angry. "I knew no good would come of you helping out at that agency. Our cousin never had a lick of sense, and you can be just as bad."

Lenore colored at the reprimand. "Mother and Father would never allow me to correspond with a man, especially a soldier . . . so I used your name." She wrung her hands and turned away from Bessie's glare. "I know it was wrong, but it seemed harmless at the time. I intended to break it off. Truly, I did. But it just escalated. He asked me to go through a proxy marriage and join him. It sounded so exciting, Bessie. I didn't think. I just did it."

She turned back and stared at Bessie with pleading eyes. "You know how I've longed for adventure, how I've dreamed of going west."

"But this, Lenore!" Bessie's heart pounded, and dread congealed in her stomach. She didn't want to think about this tangle or how on earth she would get her madcap sister out of this scrap. Their very proper parents would be horrified. They guarded their society status above all else.

Lenore slid an anxious glance at her. "Since then I met Richard. I want to be with him, not some man I've never met."

Lenore had done some thoughtless things, but this was beyond the pale. To lead a man on like this–and a soldier serving his country, no less! Despicable. Tears burned in Bessie's eyes. Would Lenore never learn to think before she leapt into things? "Are you telling me that you married this man? And falsely, too, since you aren't Bessie Randall."

Lenore couldn't meet her gaze. "No, Bessie. It means you are married to Jasper. If you contest it, I–I think I could be arrested for forging your name."

Bessie gasped. The strength ran from her legs, and she sat on the bed. Taking a deep breath, she looked from her sister back down to the tickets and the letter. She drew another shuddering breath. How was she to extricate Lenore and herself from this predicament? "I see. You didn't want to marry a man you've never met, but you've married *me* to someone I've never heard of before today." She hugged herself. "What am I to do?" she whispered. "What can be done?"

"Please don't tell Mother and Father about this. Father said if I got in any more trouble, he would ship me off to Uncle Matthew's in Rhode Island. I can't leave now that I've met Richard. I intend to marry him."

Did Lenore ever think of anyone but herself? Bessie loved her younger sister, but this was too much. She didn't know if she could forgive her this. "How could you, Lenore? How could you bind me to some man I've never met?" Her thoughts raced, trying to uncover a plan, any plan, to unravel this tangle.

Lenore burst into noisy sobs. "You hate me!"

Bessie pressed her fingers between her eyes where the persistent throbbing pulsed. "Oh, do hush, Lenore, and let me think."

Her sister's sobs tapered off, but Bessie could still feel her anxious gaze. Lenore turned away finally and began to fuss with her hair. Bessie stared at her sister. She was so lovely. Translucent skin, thick black hair, and full lips that drew men like bees to honey.

Bessie's own hair was merely mousy brown, and the rest of her features were only echoes of Lenore's beauty. Lenore had beaus by the dozen, and Bessie had yet to receive her first proposal of marriage. And she might never receive one. She wasn't ugly. Just ordinary. Quiet and ordinary.

Lenore turned from the looking glass and gave her a coaxing smile. "I know you would like Jasper. And you'd make a much better soldier's wife than I would." She crossed the room and sat on the bed beside Bessie. "You know Father says I shall not be allowed to marry until you do. What if you never marry? Richard may weary of waiting for me." She bit her lip, and tears hung on her lashes. "I don't mean to be cruel, but you're already twenty-six. Perhaps this is your opportunity."

Perhaps it was. How picky could Jasper be if he was willing to marry by proxy? Maybe he wouldn't really be expecting a beauty. Simply a wife. He was expecting Bessie Randall, and she was Bessie Randall, not Lenore. If she didn't go, she would be breaking a promise made in her name. Her reputation and honor would be smirched.

She supposed the marriage could be annulled or whatever one did in this kind of situation, but she had to be honest with herself. She longed for a husband and children of her own. Lately she had questioned whether it would ever happen—or if she would die a spinster.

"I shall never marry a nonbeliever, Lenore. What of this Jasper? Have you inquired about his faith?" That was the most important thing. She could deal with other problems, but marriage to a nonbeliever would be intolerable.

Her sister brightened. "Indeed I did. Jasper is a fine Christian man. His brother-in-law is a minister at Fort Bridger." Hope gave a sparkle to her eyes.

A minister's brother-in-law. It sounded good. Bessie pressed her fingers against the bridge of her nose again. Was this the Lord's will for her? She couldn't decide now. "I shall pray about it, Lenore. Say nothing to our parents until I make my decision." She started toward the door, then hesitated. "Have you a picture of this man? And might I see a letter or two?" Not that his looks were really important, but ill humor often showed in the expression.

"Of course." Lenore hastened to her dressing table and opened her jewel box. She extracted a photo and a bundle of letters tied with pink ribbon. "He is really a very nice man, Bessie. I think the two of you would deal splendidly together."

Bessie took the packet of letters and the photograph. "I shall be the judge of that, Lenore. Your judgment leaves much to be desired." She hardened her heart against the hurt expression on her sister's face and hurried to her own room.

After she shut the door behind her, Bessie opened the balcony door and stepped onto the small porch overlooking the ocean. Settling onto the single chair, she turned her attention first to the photograph. Jasper was not what Bessie would call handsome, but his face was interesting. A nose a bit too large for his face with a hump in the middle as though it had been broken, thick brows, and a square jaw gave his face character. And there seemed to be a bit of humor in his eyes and in the tilt of his lips. The rapid pace of her heart stilled a bit. Character was all-important. She laid the photo on the table, then untied the ribbon on the letters. She began with the oldest.

By the time she was halfway through the letters, she knew she had to go. She could not disappoint this man. She had a heart of love to give, and this man seemed willing to accept a wife with open arms. Besides, the deed was already done. She was bound to this man, and she would see it through. If he chose to put her away once he saw her, that decision would be upon his head. She would go west.

Jasper paced the rough boardwalk outside the stage depot. The stage was never on time, and today was no exception. It should have arrived early this morning, and here it was nearly five. His heart pounded at the thought of finally meeting his lovely bride. Her letters had filled him with delight, for she had a fire and passion for life. He flipped open the cover from his pocket watch again, then sighed, closed it, and slipped the watch back inside his pocket.

Stepping into the street, he looked down the rough trail to the east. Was that a cloud of dust? Shading his eyes with one hand, he squinted. It was the stage. He stepped back onto the boardwalk and slapped the dust from his breeches with his hat. What would Bessie think when she saw him? Would she be disappointed?

The lathered horses stopped in front of him, and the stagecoach driver began to toss luggage from the top of the stage to the numerous waiting hands. Someone opened the stage door, and the passengers began to disembark. A corpulent man with a handlebar mustache climbed out first, while the stage springs groaned in protest at his weight. Next came an older woman with a baby in her arms, followed by a slight young woman in drab brown.

Jasper waited eagerly for several minutes, but no one else exited. He approached the stage door and peered in: Two men in black suits were the only occupants. His heart fell. She didn't come. Her telegram had said she would be on this stage. He felt a stab of alarm. Was she all right?

The young woman in brown averted her eyes when he turned back around. She had been staring at him, and the flush on her cheeks told Jasper she was aware of her bad manners. He had to pass her to reach the telegraph office next to the stage depot, and she cleared her throat when he reached her side.

"Excuse me, sir. Are you–?" She raised grave eyes and searched his face. "Are you Jasper Mendenhall?"

He stared down at her. She was a tiny thing, barely five feet tall, and slightly built. She wore a striking hat with an ostrich feather that dangled over one eye, but such an elegant hat looked out of place on such an ordinary woman. A tendril of light-brown hair had escaped its pins and straggled against her pale cheek. Her gray eyes appeared enormous in her pinched face.

How did she know his name? A sense of unease swept over him. "Yes, ma'am. I'm Jasper Mendenhall. May I assist you in some way?"

Her lips trembled, and her face became even more colorless. She swallowed hard. "I–I'm Bessie. B–Bessie Mendenhall. Your wife."

Jasper blinked and then the breath left his lungs. This couldn't be his Bessie! His Bessie was vibrant with life. She was dark and striking. She wasn't this little mouse of a woman. Was this some kind of terrible joke?

She must have seen his shock, and tears flooded her gray eyes. She fished in her reticule but couldn't seem to find what she was looking for. "I am so sorry," she whispered. "Have you a handkerchief?"

Dazed, he pulled one from his pocket and handed it to her. He looked her over again, trying to find some resemblance to the photo he carried next to his heart. Perhaps the nose and mouth were similar?

She dabbed her cheeks, then straightened her slim shoulders and craned her head to look into his face. "Is there someplace more private we can go to discuss this matter?"

Still speechless, he nodded. He was afraid to say anything.

The hot, clamoring words rushing through his head would crush this pale creature. But he longed to shout them. Duped. He'd been duped. Jessica and Clay had been right. How could he have been so foolish? He thought he knew his Bessie, but he was obviously wrong. As he led the way down the street to Clay's church, he couldn't bear to look at her.

When he realized Bessie was nearly running to keep up with his long stride, he slowed his pace and offered her his arm. The touch of her hand on his arm was loathsome, but he forced himself to accept it. What kind of woman would deceive a man the way she'd done? Contempt curled his lip, but he kept his mouth clamped shut. He didn't dare give vent to his feelings.

He opened the church door and ushered her into the cool interior. The calming atmosphere had an immediate effect on his temper. His breathing slowed, and he seated her in a pew and stood gazing down at her.

She fiddled with the tassels on her reticule. "I know how this looks."

"Do you?"

She glanced up at his tight words. "Please, sit down. You'll give me a crick in my neck. You're very tall. Taller than I expected."

He sat beside her. "And you're not at all as I expected you."

She bit her lip. "I know. You were expecting Lenore. I didn't think to ask if she'd sent a picture of herself. When I saw your reaction, I knew she had."

"What on earth are you talking about? Who is Lenore? I don't understand anything except the fact that you deceived me."

She laid a small hand on his arm, and he had to resist the impulse to shake it off. "Lenore is my sister. My baby sister. She's twenty-one and should have known better, but she's the one who has been writing to you, using my name. I discovered these contretemps by accident, and I have come to honor the promise made in my name."

He stared into her face. Had she seriously thought that she could take the place of her lovely sister? Did she think him so desperate he would marry a bride sight unseen? Why hadn't this sister she called Lenore come? Twenty-one was of an age for marriage.

"I know how it looks." She stared down at her lap, pleating the folds of her dusty brown dress.

"I don't think you do. If you did, you wouldn't have come. You would have written and explained the situation and given me the chance to set this tangle straight. Did you think that one woman was the same as the next to me?"

"Well . . . you did write to the agency looking for a wife."

"Yes, but I had the opportunity to choose for myself." He squeezed his hands into fists. "You had a picture of me, didn't you?"

She nodded uncertainly.

"How would you have felt if you arrived and found you'd married a man of fifty with gray hair and whiskers?"

Bessie's face whitened as his words penetrated. "I see what you mean," she said softly. "You are displeased with my appearance." Tears swam in her eyes again. "Please forgive me, Lieutenant. If I'd realized you had a picture of Lenore, I can assure you I never would have come unannounced this way."

He folded his arms across his chest. "I find that hard to believe, Miss Randall." She had trapped him. Perhaps her younger sister had done it deliberately, since it was obvious she had to have known what her sister was doing.

"Mrs. Mendenhall," she corrected softly. "We are legally wed. That is why I have come."

Jasper stared at her. He wanted to groan in frustration. How could he unravel this mess? "That may be true, but under the circumstances, we may not be wed long. I will consult an attorney as soon as I can and see just where we stand."

Her face paled even more, if that were possible. "You would send me home?"

He sighed and rubbed his chin. Against his will, pity stirred his heart. Perhaps this monstrous trick was not her doing. She didn't seem conniving enough for such a scheme. "You must be tired. Let me take you to my sister's home. She likely has supper waiting."

The story continues in Colleen Coble's *To Love a Stranger* . . .

Enjoy an excerpt from Colleen Coble's

Butterfly Palace

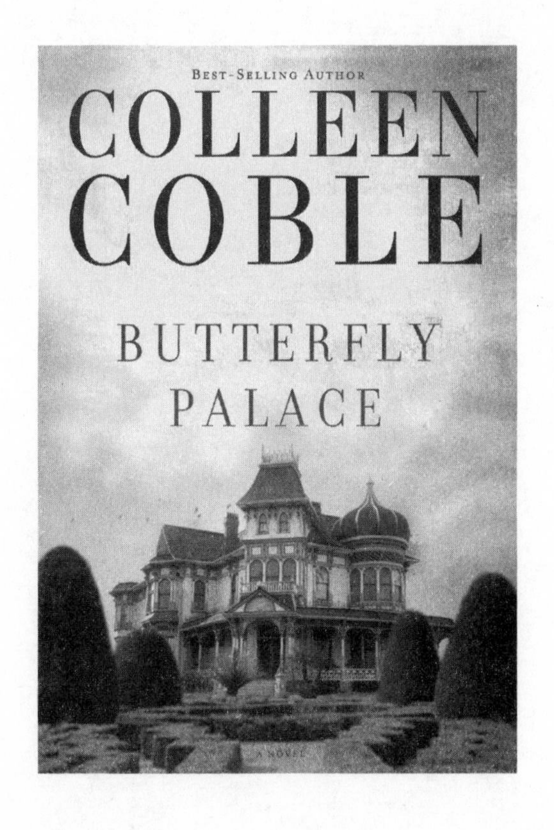

Prologue

Larson, Texas, 1900

Lily Donaldson tiptoed to the front door and winced when it opened with a creak. The last thing she wanted was to awaken her mother who was sleeping down the hall. Even though Lily was over twenty years old, her mother would take a switch to her if she knew she was sneaking out like this. The lights still shone from the livery attached to their house.

She peeked in the window as she passed. Her father sat at the desk with his partner as they pored over figures for the new expansion. There was a stack of money on the desk beside them. She stared for a moment at the stack of cash. It must have been a good day for the livery. It would be hours before their meeting came to an end. The talk of a new livery in the next town over had been going on for several weeks, and both men never seemed to tire of the topic.

The night air touched her heated skin, and she shivered as she hurried along the path to the barn. Crickets chirped as if to keep time to the ragtime tune tinkling from the tavern's piano down the street. The threat of discovery added another thump to her pulse.

The familiar scent of hay and horse greeted her when she stepped into the darkened building. "Andy?" She twisted the unfamiliar weight of the engagement ring on her finger. Her lips curved when Andy Hawkins stepped from the shadows. "I thought maybe you hadn't been able to slip away." She kept her voice barely above a whisper while she drank in his appearance.

He was a good head taller than most men, and his bulk made her feel tiny–and protected. His dark hair curled at the nape of his neck, and his eyes were the color of a buckeye nut.

His white teeth flashed below his perfect Roman nose. "I told Pa I wasn't feeling well. I'd much rather be with you." His warm hands came down on her shoulders, and he pulled her close for a kiss. "That meeting will go on for hours."

Heat ran through her at his words. She'd tried to resist the pull of their passion–they both had–but they'd been weak, so weak. The firm press of his fingers closed around her hand, and he pulled her to a comfortable stack of hay. She fell into his arms without a protest. His lips came down on hers, and she forgot everything but his touch.

He lifted his head and sniffed. "Do you smell smoke?"

Cries of alarm began to filter into her consciousness, muddied by the feel and scent of Andy. He helped her to her feet, and they both rushed to the door to view a scene that made her shudder.

Fire shot through the roof of the livery. "Pa!" Andy restrained her when she would have rushed forward.

More shouts came from town, and a line of men burst from the saloon and ran toward the burning building. The windows of the livery exploded, spewing broken glass onto the ground, then smoke poured from open frames.

Andy grabbed her hand, and they ran toward her front door.

She stopped and stared at the fire. Which direction? Her mother was in the house. Their fathers were in the livery. Lily's chest was tight as flames consumed the livery.

Her fingers closed around the doorknob. "I'll get my mother. You get the men." The metal was already hot to the touch. How could the fire have grown so quickly?

She yanked open the door and plunged inside. Thick, roiling smoke choked Lily's nose and throat as soon as she reached the top of the stairs. She threw open the bedroom door and rushed to the bed. The smoke was thick in the bedroom too. Her mother slept, unaware of the danger.

Lily shook her. "Mama, wake up! You have to get out of here." Shouts and screams echoed from outside. What was happening to her father?

Her mother lifted her head and her eyes went wide, then cleared of confusion. She threw back the covers, then stumbled to the door with Lily. One hand around her mother's waist, Lily led her down the steps. Her chest burned both with the hot smoke and the need to escape.

"Almost there," she told her mother. She reached blindly for the door, and her fingers grasped the knob. She threw open the door.

The first brush of fresh air on her skin made her gasp and

draw in the thick smoke. She coughed at the searing pain in her chest, then stumbled onto the porch with her mother. Lily led her mother a safe distance away before turning to see bright flames shooting into the night. A fire alarm clanged behind them, and the horses pulling the fire engine raced around the corner. As soon as it came to a stop, the firemen leaped into the yard and ran for the livery.

Her mother coughed and stared at the furiously burning structure. "Where's your father?"

But Lily didn't see her father's bald head. Dread congealed in her belly, and she shook her head. "I don't see them, but Andy went to get them out." She stared at the throng around the building. Was that Andy?

His soot-blackened face came into view by the light of the flames. He struggled with the two men holding him. "Let go of me! I have to find them."

"It's too dangerous," one of the men said. "The place is fully engulfed."

"Stay here, Mama." Lily hurried to Andy's side. "You didn't find them?" Her throat closed at the hopeless expression on his face.

She turned to stare at the inferno that had overrun both the livery and the attached house. The fire's heat scorched her face. The breeze blew stinging cinders against her skin. Andy renewed his efforts to free himself, but the firemen propelled him back to a safer distance.

The fire's roar was like a dragon from a fairy tale, monstrous and all-consuming. Flames licked out of the upper windows, straining toward the roof. More glass shattered, and the stink of burning bedding rolled over the lawn. With a groan, the building began to sag. The firemen shoved them back even more, and they all turned to watch it give a final shudder before the weakened timbers collapsed. Sparks and flames shot higher as the fire fed on the night air and began to consume the last of the building.

Lily sank to her knees, and Andy fell with her. They held one another as the fire took their fathers.

Andy stiffened, then pulled away. "It's my fault. I should have been there. I would have smelled it and gotten them out."

"It went too fast, Andy. There was nothing any of us could do." She tried to cup his face in her hands, but he flinched away, then jumped to his feet.

"Don't look at me. I can't even stand myself." He stalked off, and the dark swallowed him up.

One

Austin, Texas, 1904

The train's whistle sounded as mournful as she felt as it pulled away from the station, leaving her on the siding with her valise at her feet. Lily brushed ineffectively at the soot on her serviceable gray skirt and squinted in the October sunshine. What if her new employer had sent no one to meet her? She didn't know how to get to her destination.

A dray pulled by two fine horses went past, and the driver stared too boldly for her taste, so she directed her gaze to her dusty black boots.

"Miss?"

She jerked her gaze back up to see a man dressed in a brown suit. A lock of reddish hair dipped below his stylish bowler. He appeared to be in his late thirties and was quite handsome.

He tipped his hat and nodded toward her luggage. "Is that all you have? You *are* Lily Donaldson?"

"Yes, yes, I am. You are from the Butterfly Palace?"

He picked up her valise and gave a vague nod her way. "This way."

People flowed around her as she followed his broad back to a fine automobile at the street. She hung back when he opened the door. "You didn't mention your name."

Amusement lit his pale blue eyes. "I'm not the killer attacking women here if that's what you're worried about."

She glanced around at the men loitering nearby. No one seemed to pay her any notice. "There's a killer?"

He shrugged. "A city is never as safe as it looks. Are you coming or not? I don't care either way. Mother asked me to fetch you when I objected to being forced to attend another of her boring balls, and I obliged. It's on your own head if you're late."

When he started for the driver's seat, she hoisted herself onto the plush seat. "I'm coming."

He grinned, and heat flared in her cheeks at his bold stare. His expensive suit proclaimed him to be much more than a driver sent to collect her. He'd mentioned his mother, so she assumed he was a Marshall.

The jerk of the automobile threw her against the leather seat and ended her speculation. It felt good to be away from the curious stares she'd endured on the train. Women didn't travel alone. She took off her bonnet and swiped some loose strands back into place, then replaced her hat.

She stared eagerly out the window at Austin. The state capital. It was much grander than she'd imagined. Electric trolley cars zipped by so fast they made her woozy. Houses larger than four or five homes back in Larson turned stately faces toward the wide street. Mercantile shops, printers, meat markets, and dress shops passed in a dizzying blur. Where did one start to find needed items? There were too many shops to choose from.

The scent of lilacs blew away the stench of the train's coal dust that lingered on her clothing. Her pulse beat hard and fast in her neck. Her new life was about to begin, and she had no idea what to expect. While she hoped to find a new life here, the recent death of her mother left her expecting only more heartache. Still, she had to support herself even if life seemed hard and dreary.

Didn't God care? She'd never expected him to let such terrible things happen. Ever since the fire, life had spiraled down in a disheartening whirlpool of pain.

The automobile stopped in front of a grand stone mansion illuminated by electric lights. The cobblestone drive was smooth under her shoes when the man assisted her out of the back. Lily stood, absorbing the huge edifice that would have been more at home on a French mountainside. Seeing it here on Texas soil felt wrong somehow, and something about the structure was off-putting in spite of its grandeur. Maybe it was the way the windows in the mansard roof seemed to leer down at her, or perhaps it was the dark brick that made it look stern and unwelcoming. A chill shuddered down her spine, but she picked up her valise. It would surely be more attractive in the daylight.

The man shut the automobile door behind her. "Welcome to Butterfly Palace, Lily."

His forwardness in addressing her by her Christian name made her straighten. "Why is it called that?" She craned her neck again and willed herself to admire the four-story mansion.

"My stepfather is a great collector of exotic butterflies. He employs a man to bring him the finest in the world. The sunroom is filled with them, and frescoes can be found everywhere." He pointed. "You'll want to go around back to the staff entrance, but I'm sure we'll be seeing more of one another. The name's Lambreth. I suppose I'll inherit this monstrosity someday." He winked at her.

The instructions and his wink took her aback. There was little distinction between servant and master in Larson, but then, no one in her hometown put on airs or flashed their wealth around. She took a step toward the side of the house, but Mr. Lambreth touched her arm and motioned her in the other direction.

"I'll have Rollo bring in your trunk. Mrs. O'Reilly will tell you where you're sleeping. See you around."

"Thank you." Gathering her courage, Lily followed a cobblestone path around the west side of the house.

Light spilled into a rose garden from large windows along the side of the house. Lily stopped and gaped. Women in shimmering silk dresses mingled with men in formal attire under a spectacular gas chandelier. The opulent scene was like something from *Godey's*. Houseboys and maids carrying trays offered food and drink to the guests, and piano music tinkled out the open windows.

She reined in her impulse to run back to the automobile and ask to be returned to the train. This life was far outside her experience, and she'd never fit in here. Would she be expected to wear a black dress and white apron and cap?

Tightening her grip on her small valise, she forced herself forward to the back door. The aroma of roast beef mingled with fish and cake as she knocked on the door.

The door opened, and a slim woman about Lily's age peered out. Her hazel eyes sparkled with life above flushed cheeks. "You must be Lily. I expected you an hour ago. We need you." She reached out and yanked the valise from Lily's hand. "We're shorthanded. Your dress will do for now, but take off your hat and put on an apron."

She left the door standing open and stepped back into a hall that opened into a large kitchen. Lily followed the young woman into the kitchen where the cooking odors grew stronger. The aromas of beef and fish vied with that of cinnamon and apples. Food covered a scarred wooden table, and several servants bustled around the room.

A tiny woman dressed in black orchestrated the chaos. The red hair under her cap was coiled in a bun tight enough to give her a headache. Her brown eyes assessed Lily, and she nodded. "So you're Lily?" Her brogue told of her Irish heritage. "I'm Glenda O'Reilly, the housekeeper. You may call me Mrs. O'Reilly."

"What would you have me do tonight?"

Mrs. O'Reilly pointed to a shelf and pegs. "Hang up your hat there. Emily, get her an apron."

The young woman who had opened the door nodded and reached into a cupboard. She handed a white apron to Lily. "You can take around the cider."

Lily pulled the pins from her hat and placed it on the shelf, then tied the apron around her waist. "You're Emily?"

The young woman nodded. "Sorry, love, I didn't introduce myself, did I? We'll be roommates, and there will be time to get acquainted later. *After* the party."

Lily's chest felt tight, and she wished she'd hidden out in the rose garden until the party was over. "When am I to meet Mrs. Marshall?"

"Tomorrow." Mrs. O'Reilly's brow lifted in challenge as if daring Lily to object.

"Yes, ma'am. I am just to offer the guests cider? I'll do my best."

"That's all I ask." The housekeeper pointed to a large tray filled with fine blue-and-white china cups. "Smile and let the guests take their own cup of mulled cider. Try not to spill it. When your tray is empty, come back here and get more."

Like Joan of Arc going to the stake, Lily squared her shoulders and picked up the tray.

Women in shimmering silks of every imaginable color danced by on the arms of men in sleek black suits. A mural over the fireplace depicted a butterfly in beautiful hues of blue and yellow. Drew Hawkes hung back in the corner and idly listened to the conversations around him, mostly about the recent murder of a servant girl. The unfortunate young woman had been discovered a few blocks from here, and the entire city was in a state. This was the third murder in two months.

Everett Marshall motioned to Drew, and he left the sanctuary of his corner to join him. Everett clapped a hand on Drew's shoulder. "This is the young man I was telling you about. Drew is quite gifted with investments, and you would do well to employ him.

Drew, this is Stuart Vesters. He owns the stockyard on the west side of town." Drew shook the man's hand, noticing the lack of enthusiasm in Stuart's grip. "Pleased to meet you, Mr. Vesters. I'm not currently taking on more clients though, sir. I'd be happy to put you on a waiting list." Dangling the carrot just out of reach tended to be much more effective than a hard sell.

Sure enough, the older man squared his shoulders and lifted a brow. "When could we discuss it, Mr. Hawkes? I might be persuaded to change investment companies. Everett here has been singing your praises for more than a month."

"I'm booked through the next three weeks, but I'd be happy to make an appointment after Thanksgiving." Drew had been trying to get close to Vesters for nearly six months. It wouldn't do to appear too eager. His supervisor wouldn't be happy if he ruined things now.

"That's much too far. I have some time on Thursday. We can meet in town."

Drew eyed the man's set jaw and read his determination. Good. "Let me see if I can rearrange my schedule." He whipped out a black leather calendar and pretended to peruse it. He pulled out a pencil and acted as though he were erasing something. "I can make that work. My other client may squawk, but I'll make it up to him with a new tip."

Vesters smiled with self-satisfaction, and Drew allowed himself a small smile as the man reached for a glass of cider. Drew looked at the young woman holding the tray. He blinked and looked again. All the blood drained from his head, and his knees went weak as he took in the blond hair and pointed chin.

Lily? It wasn't possible. She hadn't seen him yet as her attention was on Vesters. Drew's gaze drank in the face he'd seen only in his dreams for four years. Those delicate features and smooth skin hadn't changed in all this time. Her eyes were such a dark blue, and they grew even darker when she was angry. The glorious hair he'd loved to see released from its pins was hidden under an ugly maid's cap. The years had brought a new maturity to her beauty.

Drew turned on his heels and melted into the crowd. His pulse throbbed in his throat. He had to calm himself. If Vesters smelled something off now, it could ruin the whole thing. He spared a glance back at the group, but she wasn't looking his way. Maybe she hadn't seen him.

What was Lily doing here, so far from Larson? She wore an apron like she was a maid. Part of him longed to rush to her and announce himself. Did she hate him? He deserved it after the way he'd left without a word.

He was in the middle of the dancing couples, so he cut in on the man squiring Belle Castle. "I hope you don't mind, Miss Castle."

"Not at all, Mr. Hawkes." She flashed him a coy smile.

He'd known for weeks that the beautiful brunette held some fondness for him, and he hated to encourage it now, but Everett would be happy to see him dancing with his niece and would unlikely be upset at Drew's sudden departure. Everett would smooth things over with Vesters.

Drew was so distracted he didn't notice when the musicians struck up a reel. Belle picked up her pace but he didn't. Their feet became entangled. He tried to catch his balance, but everything was happening too fast. He released Belle so she wouldn't share his disgrace. In the moment he scrambled away, his arm collided with the soft body of someone behind him. The deep red Oriental rug rose to meet him, and they both went down in a tangle of limbs. The contents of the china cups darkened the red carpet to deep garnet.

The rest of the dancers stopped and stared. Someone snickered, and heat rose to his face. He quickly flipped the lady's dress over her lower limbs and sprang to his feet. "I'm terribly sorry. I–I–" His apology died when he stared into Lily's scarlet face.

Her eyes were wide and horrified. "Andy?"

He hadn't heard that nickname since his father died. "I'll explain later," he said low enough that only she could hear. After helping her to her feet, he knelt and put the cups back on the tray. Some of them were broken, and he prayed she wasn't blamed for the encounter.

She hadn't left when he stood with the tray in his hands. The rest of the guests began to move off, and the music tinkled out again.

Knowing his duty, he glanced at Belle. "I'm so sorry, Miss Castle. You are unharmed?"

"I'm fine, Mr. Hawkes." Belle smiled, and the amusement

lit her eyes with a warm glow. "That was a much-needed bit of excitement for this too-dull party. I do believe I'll take my leave though and attend to my dress." She gestured to dark splotches on her gown. He opened his mouth to apologize again, but she held up her hand. "No harm done. I'll see you tomorrow for dinner."

He gave a slight bow. "I shall look forward to it."

Christopher Lambreth, Mrs. Marshall's son, gave a genial grin and held out his arm. "I'll escort you, cousin. I fear you've lost your usual fine sense of balance."

Belle laughed and took his arm. When her emerald skirt disappeared in the swirl of other gowns, Drew turned his attention back to Lily. She seemed rooted to the spot. His reappearance had to have rattled her.

He took her arm. "Let's get out of here. Make no sign that you know me."

She gave a slight nod. "Your past actions have already made it clear I don't know you at all."

His lips tightened, and he guided her through the crowd to the blessed cool of the hall outside the ballroom. "Lily, what are you doing here?"

She jerked her arm from his grip. "I think the better question would be, what are *you* doing here, Andy? And the first question begs the second. Where have you been for the past four years and two months?"

Part of him rejoiced that she knew so clearly how long he'd been gone, but that fact also revealed the depth of the pain he'd caused. "It will take too long to explain now. Can you meet me tomorrow afternoon at the park? Say nothing about my identity to anyone."

She shook her head. "I don't think I want to hear it. And besides, I don't know what my duties are yet. I just arrived tonight." Her eyes filled with tears. "Who are you really, Andy?" She turned toward the kitchen door.

"Wait, Lily, I want to talk to you." But the swish of her skirt was the only response he received.

The story continues in Colleen Coble's *Butterfly Palace*...

A Journey *of the* Heart

Enjoy the entire colection as an e-bundle.
Individual titles available in print only.

9780529103413-A

Colleen loves to hear from her readers!

Be sure to sign up for Colleen's newsletter for insider information on deals and appearances.

Visit her website at www.colleencoble.com
Twitter: @colleencoble
Facebook: colleencoblebooks

Thomas Nelson
Since 1798